T.

GRETA YANCEY

SAGA

Thomas Buckskin Publishing

P.O. Box 675
St. Helen, MI 48656

uka,
Happy 9th Birthday!
Love nomie

ELIZABETH M. DUNAJ

THE GRETA YANCEY SAGA

Book Three

ACROSS THE PRAIRIE

Cover Illustrated

By

ROSE MARIE SCHERER

ALYSSA PRENTICE

Thomas Buckskin Publishing

P.O. Box 675
St. Helen, MI 48656

ISBN: 978-0-615-42240-4

Library of Congress Control Number: 2010941281

Thomas Buckskin Publishing, Saint Helen, Michigan 48656

DEDICATION

I dedicate this book to God first who gave me the talent to do all that I do! ". . . but with God all things are possible." Matthew 19:26

To Jim, my fantastic husband, for standing by me and supporting me with encouraging words and for not telling what happens in the books. Jim continues to be surrounded by my readers wanting to know when the next book will be out. You are my gem! I love you! Thank you!

To my Children, their Spouses, my Grandchildren, all who have been great supporters! Thank you!

To Relatives, Friends and Fans who have patiently waited for this third book. Here it is. Enjoy! Thank you for your support!

A special thanks to Deloris and Rose Marie for taking time to proof read my book, you arc the greatest! Thank you!

CHARACTERS

Greta Yancey: Widow Mother of seven daughters

Daughter's: Eldest to youngest, all play piano and fiddle

Emma — runs the farm with her mother

Ruth — loves to bake and cook

Claire — takes care of the horses

Anne — sews the best stitch

Katie — does not like change

Alex — loves caring for animals and people

Marie — adventurous

Ellie Cooper — Greta's best friendship

Doctor William Allen — Hometown Doctor, also known as "Doc"

Matthew (Matt) Braummer — Man in love with Greta; Saloon owner in Earleysburg, Penn.; Whispering Oaks Plantation in Louisiana

Tom (Coop) Cooper — Son of Ellie. Mountain Man

Brave Eagle — Best friend of Tom, Lakota (Sioux) Indian

Louisiana Characters

Emily Braummer — Matthew's sister who lives on the Whispering Oaks Plantation.

Minton — Main Housekeeper & Cook

Able — Main House Servant

Horse Names & Owners

Tilley & Tabby — colors bay & brown ~ Greta

Misty — color grey ~ Ellie

Blizzard — color white ~ Emma

Freckles — color chestnut ~ Ruth

Appleseed — color brown ~ Claire

Buttercup — color cream ~ Anne

Chewy — color blonde ~ Katie

Jade — color very dark brown ~ Alex

Maximus — color black ~ Marie

Clyde — color brown ~ Doc Allen

Blackjack — color black ~ Matt

Moose — color brown ~ Tom Cooper

Misun (little brother) - color black and white ~ Brave Eagle

Buckshot — color black and grey ~ Isaac

A LITTLE INFORMATION

Scripture, taken from the King James Bible (Hebrew/ Greek Study Bible, and the Revised King James Bible (copyright 1970, 1973).

In the 1800's recipes were referred to as "receipt".

In the 1800's people spoke a little different than what we do now. The wording and dialog may not be like ours in some areas of the story.

Bacon was called ham by the English or "sow-belly" by the pioneers.

"Slam-John" was flapjacks, better known as pancakes.

I mainly write in the present tense—everything in the "now" and moving forward.

... The saga continues ...

CHAPTER ONE

The four days passed quickly since the attack of the Prairie Banditos.

The route took a westerly destination continuing on the northern side of the Missouri River. Their first stop after the attack was a two and a half day trip to Fulton. There they replenished what was needed and left early morning. Their plans to stop at Liberty took them past Columbia, Franklin, Charion, and Bluffton. The area traveled consisted of bluffs, trees, flat areas, and little streams. Injuries had held them up long enough and Mr. Josiah MacGhie with all do respect for the injured ones insisted on pushing to the next town and camping outside each town until they reach Liberty. The girls gave no fuss as they had all agreed Mr. MacGhie would take full control of their travels. Though the ladies would have loved to explore each town, they realized they were not on a site seeing adventure and must forgo any side excursions.

The group traveled about 12 to 15 miles per day depending on the activity of the day and the weather; as nice weather meant longer days travel. The rain made it harder for travel. The smaller wagon belonging to Isaac and Alex would sink deep in the soft watery mud on numerous occasions. While the heavy rain continued to pour down it took a lot of effort on the horses working hard to get a grip, and the men as they tried to get a foothold in this mud that would suck the boots in place not wanting to let go. They pushed and pulled to get the wheels moving. The men often lost their foothold and fell into the mud only to get up and try again. Finally, after fighting this gushy mud, the men won and the wagon was on a roll again. They beat the thick prairie mud once again that wanted to hold its captives forever.

After the rain, the road traveled was equally as rough as rain run-offs made grooves in the ground traveled and riding in a wagon was not comfortable. Greta had no choice in the matter as her injuries called for bed rest and the girls did all they could think of to make their mother and two sisters, Katie and Ruth, comfortable. They had all the quilts and some blankets padded in the backside of one of the wagons, making sure to pad in their mother extra well. They made sure nothing was overhead that might fall on the injured travelers as the wagon bounced and swayed with each rut and bump. To give more comfort to the injured ones Emma placed a rifle along the back of the wagon. As they cared for the injured the daily routine was always the same regardless of weather; early to rise, prepare meals, tend to the animals, changing the order of the wagons from time to time, sometimes wagons road side by side. The night was no different on the open prairie from any other night. Wagons were circled, the large workhorses that worked hard daily were unhitched, fires built, tents put up, mules were unloaded of their packs. The travelers resembled little ants' busy going about the necessary duties to make a comfortable camp. Everyone had a job to complete before they could relax.

"Tom!" yelled Josiah MacGhie, leader of the Fur Company, consisting of Free Trappers who owed allegiance to no single company. This was their Fur Company. "We will hold up here for the night. Inform the ladies please and meet me by the mules."

Tom informed the ladies and then returned to where they were unloading the mules for the night.

"What did you need Josiah?" Tom said as he began to untie the bundles on a mule. Brave Eagle was there already unloading the mules.

"Looks like the ladies are traveling well. I have not heard any complaints, have you?" Josiah said as he stacked bundles to one side.

"No, and Emma would be the one to let us know if her mother needed extra stopping. I do believe those ladies will fair well on this trip no matter what comes against them." Tom said smiling.

"I agree with you on that. Welp, another days ride and we should be in Liberty. We can stay a couple days then on to Cantonment Leavenworth."

"Sounds good to me, Josiah." Tom said as Brave Eagle agrees.

"Yes I thought so to, thanks for confirming it. I will inform your mother of what to expect ahead of us and then get this group bedded down." Josiah said as he mounted his horse.

"Hey Josiah, I thought your group takes a steamboat to Leavenworth then the rest of the way on foot. You miss your boat?" Tom smiled.

"Yupe, seems some pretty skirts needed us more than we needed the boat ride." Josiah said as he turned his horse toward Mrs. Cooper.

"I hear you loud and clear." Tom said giving a waive. When done he mounted his horse and rode up to Marie who was unhitching the front team and said, "Need a helping hand there little lady?"

"Oh Mr. Tom, I sure could use your help. These horses are great but so darn big I have a time getting them unhitched and ready for the night. And six horses each wagon, golly, at the rate I am going I will probably get finished in time to hitch them up again." Marie said as she struggled getting the harness off the head of *Whisper*.

Brave Eagle, smiling, dismounts and begins to unhitch the horses on another wagon.

"Yes these horses are big." He looks back at the two that are right in front of the wagon. "What are they about seventeen hands high, weighing in at every bit of eighteen hundred pounds. Nevertheless, Marie, these horses are the best for this kind of travel being well muscled and having the longest stride that could cover about fifteen miles a day. Your Ma set them up right too."

"How do you mean?" Marie asked as she backed up and allowed Tom to remove the harness.

"She placed the heaviest horses nearest the wagon because they have the job of turning the wagons and backing them up. That is why *Champ* and *Corny* are placed where they are, their both good strong horses. In addition, they get along with most any horse you put them with. In fact looking over all these horses that are wagon pullers . . . yupe . . . your Ma is a good one. These horses are pretty much docile and steady, good temperament."

"Oh I always thought the lead horses did all the work but these back horses actually do the pulling and pushing." Marie said as she led *Whisper* away from the wagon and began unhitching *Blue*, the first two horses.

"That is exactly right Marie. Look at the size of *Whisper* compared to *Champ*, you see how much bigger and stronger *Champ* looks than *Whisper*?"

"Yes I do see the difference Mr. Tom. I never noticed it before and Ma would have us girls ride *Champ* or one of the other back horses on the left side when no one was sitting up on the bench."

"Yupe, these back horses are the heaviest and best horses to do the job. When we get this team unhitched I will help you brush them down and hobble them." Tom said as he worked to remove the rest of the harness from the other horses.

"Thank you Mr. Tom, this is a big job, but these horses deserve the extra attention. I know they are loyal to the family."

"All horses are loyal to their owners as long as they are treated right." Tom smiled then said, "Now let's get to brushing."

"You know Mr. Tom, I was thinking about Mr. Hawthorn, the blacksmith back home. He fixed the front of the wagons for us to sit on like a regular wagon and I am glad for that."

"Why is that Marie?"

Wrinkling her nose she says, "Because, I would not want to sit on that lazy board to guide the horses. I like sitting on top where you can see everything in front of you and all around you."

"That is good thinking. But you know, the men who drive these teams hauling supplies all ride on that lazy board on the left side of the wagon and have no problems." Tom said with a smile.

"Well, I am not one of them and I like being high on top."

Tom laughed and they continued to brush down and care for the horses. A few of the men from the fur company joined them and that made Marie even happier.

When the horses were taken care of Marie went to eat.

After Emma completed her tasks she walked over to her mother as a gentle breeze began to move through the trees. A refreshing breeze that gives a soothing feeling when passing by, she said, "Mother are you comfortable?"

"As best as can be. I will be hurting no matter where I lay. Katie, Ruth how are you doing?"

"Sure could go for a hot cup of tea, if you have a mind to make some Emma." Ruth said.

"For me too, please." Katie said as she slowly adjusted herself.

"I will be back with tea for you all. But first Claire and I will help you to the tent. Think you could sit a while to eat and drink your tea Ma?" Emma said as she dropped the back of the wagon gate.

"Yes I think I can." Greta said as she slowly moved herself toward the edge of the opening.

"I will get Claire and be right back." Emma said and her Mother smiled in agreement.

Greta was looking at the sky as darkness blanketed them saying, "Look at all the stars. This sky is so big. It never ends, and what a welcoming breeze."

The three gaze out the back of the wagon at the vast black sky covered with tiny twinkling lights while enjoying the gentle breeze against their faces and arms. As they did so, Doc walked up and questioned them on their injuries suggesting they try to sleep in the tent on something flat for a change to give their body a good rest. When Emma returned, she and Claire helped their mother and sisters to the closest tent.

Marie brought in their tea and Anne brought them steaming bowls of stew with a couple of biscuits. The girls then returned to the fire to finish their meal with Alex and Isaac. Some of the men were singing around their fire and one was playing a harmonica. It was very soothing not only to the animals but also to the weary travelers. It did not take long for the girls to get comfortable in the tent. Emma and Claire helped move their mother to a cot for her to lie on. Greta welcomed the softness of the cot that was padded with quilts.

Emma grabbed her Bible and asked her mother what she would like to hear.

"Romans 15." Greta commented.

"Alright Mother, Romans 15 *'We then that are strong ought to bear the infirmities of the weak, and not to please ourselves. Let every one of us please his neighbor for his good to edification. For even Christ pleased not himself; but, as it is written, the reproaches of them that reproached thee fell on me. For whatsoever things were written aforetime were written for our learning, that we through patience and comfort of the scriptures might have hope. Now the God of patience and consolation grant you to be likeminded one toward another according to Christ Jesus: That ye may with one mind and one mouth glorify God, even the Father of our Lord Jesus Christ."* Emma yawns and glances at her mother who is sleeping. "Come on girls lets get some sleep too. I can finish reading tomorrow night. Good night." Emma says as she marks her place in her Bible. The girls return the same and in a short time all are sleeping.

Now in the early morning they approach Liberty, Missouri, a town of considerable size that is a steamboat port. Most of the town was laid out to the south and east of town leaving the open fields to the north and west for farming. Liberty brings the tired travelers about 170 miles since the attack, a town in which they all wanted to take a needed rest.

Emma and Marie ride along side one another guiding the cattle in the direction they should go and gazing their eyes on the many steamboats that were docking and leaving port to unknown destinations and discussing how helpful people have been.

Ellic rode up along side of them saying, "Mr. MacGhie will be sending one of his men up here to show you where the cattle will stay when we get into Liberty. Please follow his directions."

"Yes Ma'am. We were talking about all that we had gone through. I do not know what we would have done without the help of these men." Emma said.

"And we cannot forget the help of Isaac's family. We have a great deal to be thankful for." Ellie replied.

"We cannot forget Doc and Mr. Braummer. They helped just as much as Mr. Cooper and Mr. Brave Eagle."

"Yes Marie they sure did. We indeed have much to be grateful for. Here comes one of the men . . . pay attention to his instructions." Ellie said as she rode away. The girls nod and listen to the instructions for the cattle and follow the man.

Arriving at Liberty, crowds of people were everywhere and a decision needs to be made.

Mr. MacGhie approaches Ellie saying, "I am not sure we should stay here Ma'am. Looks like trouble."

"What do you mean?"

"Ma'am, with all do respect these people are talking about the Mormons and wanting them out of here. We could get caught up in something that would be hard to walk away from."

"I am sorry but I do not understand what you mean."

"Well Ma'am. These Mormons have their own way of doing things and they have their own quest. The main thing is they do not believe in slavery and have been meeting a lot with certain Indian tribes. And these Mormons follow their own book of Mormons which causes great fights. Now, Ma'am as far as I am concerned I choose to follow God's Holy Bible, the whole thing and having Jesus as my Savior. Plus, I do not get mixed up in a fight already happening. That's what the good book says and I listen. I do not cotton to slavery either but this state does. Around here, folks just do not tolerate these Mormons. People are against this group to the depths of tar and feathering their leaders. No Ma'am, we best get what we need and push on ahead and let this town do what it will. I know everyone is tired and wished to stay here but I think this is best for all."

"Yes I see what you mean. I will check with the girls to see if there is anything needed and get right. . . " Suddenly they hear a commotion and stopped talking.

Groups of men were shouting as they approached the wagon where Greta, Katie, and Ruth were resting. "Look there, more Mormons coming in! You part of this Mormon group? We do not want you here! Get out!"

Greta leans up and is stunned to see angry men with clubs and whips yelling as they approach her wagon. She finds the rifle just as Emma rides up on her horse quickly putting herself between her mother, sisters, and the angry men saying, "Just what do you think you are doing? Do not disturb my mother and sisters with your shouting! Leave our wagon at once or I will start shooting!"

Ellie and Mr. MacGhie quickly head to the wagon to quiet things down. MacGhie comes between Emma and the angered mob of men saying, "I am Josiah MacGhie leader of this Fur Company and traveling with these wagons. May I help you?" Matt and Doc approach the group after hearing the loud shouting and listen to the conversation with hands on their pistols prepared for anything.

"You shore can. You all belong to these Mormons? Denounce the Book of Mormon or leave this county!"

"No Sir we are not Mormons. We are simply travelers heading to Fort William and thought we would stay the night. However . . . we have decided to move on. Now, please go about your own business and leave us to ours. We will be gone within the hour."

"Well, if you are not one of them Mormons then you might as well bed down here for the night. You will not be disturbed. Course your men may be needed to give a hand in the night."

"Thank you Sir but no, we will move on."

"Suit yourself. Come on men there are other wagons over there let's check 'em out!"

McGhie shouts to the mob, "Those other four wagons belong to this group. Leave 'em alone!"

The angered men listen and they are heard grumbling as they go their way.

Emma looks at Ellie and Mr. MacGhie saying, "What was that all about? I was ready to shoot at them. Mother are you alright?"

"Yes I am. What is going on?" Greta said as she lays the rifle back down.

Ellie and Mr. MacGhie fill them in and Emma quickly checks with the girls to see what they need. She was happy to report that they needed nothing and would take the wagons and animals out of this town and wait for the rest of the group to catch up. All agreed and they moved out as fast as they could before any more trouble came their way. Matt and Doc rode off to inform Cooper and Brave Eagle of what took place and the decision to leave.

About fifteen miles away from town, they made camp in a little cove of trees. Night was coming in fast and time to get settled was short. The weather showed to be favorable for the travelers.

Greta, Ruth, and Katie stayed in the wagon as usual while the others bedded down under the huge wagons. Mr. MacGhie informed them that they would stay one more night in the area that proved to be safe then they would push onward to Cantonment Leavenworth.

The cove of trees added shade and comfort and in the morning, the sun was warming the ground. Matt was busy fixing up an area for Greta to relax in. He found a very nice spot under some trees on a little knoll where she could relax and watch the camp. The sky was a deep blue with cotton ball clouds lazily moving along. Matt rode up to Greta's wagon saying, "Good morning Mrs. Yancey. How are you?"

"Good morning Mr. Braummer. I have finally been able to sleep through the night. The girls have truly padded me in right comfortable . . . for the most part. Well, Mr. Braummer, how have you been? I have not seen much of you lately?"

"I have been helping the girls with the animals. Also unloading and loading the pack mules with Doc."

"I see."

"Yes well . . . MacGhie says we will leave tomorrow. Now, if you will allow me." Matt dismounts and ties his horse up to the one side of the wagon. He continues, "I fixed up a nice spot under some trees for you to relax under while Ellie is making breakfast." Matt unhooks the back of the wagon and takes her to the trees, sitting her on a blanket that was spread out and part way up the tree so Greta could lean against it. "There you go. Comfortable?"

"Yes thank you. The fresh air and slight breeze feels very good. If only my head would just stop hurting I think I would feel much better."

"I did not know your head was still hurting. I am sorry to hear that. Have this cup of cool water and when Ellie gets the coffee done I will bring you a cup."

"Thank you. I am thinking that either that Indian hit me on the head or when my head hit the ground. Either way, it really is hurting." She says as she touches the side of her head.

"Would you like me to get Doc?" Matt says placing his hand on hers.

"No, I do not think he can do much. We just have to wait until the injuries go away."

As Greta sips the cool water, commenting on how good it tastes, she watches as the girls help their injured sisters to sit by the fire pit and the men taking care of the animals. Matt begins talking, "Greta . . . we have so much to talk about and plans to make and . . . why I was even telling Doc some of my plans and. . . "

Greta stops drinking the water and looks at him confused saying, "Plans? What plans?"

"Plans of us." Matt says as he kneels next to her, his heart pounding, as he is full of happiness and excitement his smile couldn't get any bigger.

"Us?"

"Yes. Preacher Anderson said. . . "

She interrupts again. "Us? Preacher Anderson?"

"Yes, as I was saying. . . "

"Mr. Braummer. I cannot think of us at all. I do not know why you came all the way out here from Earelysburg . . . although I am very grateful, none the less, I need to think of my girls, our wounds healing and. . . "

A bit frustrated Matt continues, "Mrs. Yancey . . . Greta, I understand all that you are saying and I know your girls are your first thoughts and the cabin . . . but dang it woman . . . there is also me and in my life you are a very big part of it—"

"No Sir! There cannot be a, you and me! I have a lot to do before I even think of a possible you and me!"

"What! Why? What is it Greta? A person just does not have this strong of a conviction to get to a certain place or to take care of others above everything else! Now you and me . . . we have somewhat of a history and. . . "

"Stop right there Mr. Braummer! History? I do not think so. And there will be no history discussion!"

"Our history needs to be discussed and now is as good a time as ever, Mrs. Yancey!"

"Oh . . . oh alright . . . now! Right now! Yes, maybe you can finally explain a few things. History . . . like when I went to visit my sister, whom I happened to have told all about you . . . then . . . then I return home to have Seth tell me . . . on the very day of my return, he tells me you moved to Louisiana to help your sister Emily on your plantation!"

Matt attempts to say something but Greta cuts him off and continues as she points her finger at him and waving her arms, "Do not say a word till I am done! You knew I just went for a visit! Seth tells me that you told him I moved back to my sisters and you were going to your sister, and that we decided to part company! Part company! However, Mr. Braummer, we did not decide that and you lied! If you did not want to marry me, all you had to do was say so! I was so angered at you, no, do not speak . . . history you want and history you will get! I was so very angry with you and hurt that when Seth asked me to marry him I said yes . . . do you understand that? I said yes to a man I did not love! I did not love Seth . . . I loved you! After that nothing mattered until my girls came along!"

Matt says, "May I speak now?"

Greta wipes her eyes and nods her head saying, "The history lesson continues."

He took a deep breath, not even sure she would accept what he has to say, "Greta . . . Seth knew I was going to ask you to marry me. . . "

"Oh! Is that right . . . that is why. . . "

"Greta! Please, I listened to you, please listen to me."

Throwing down her cup of water and folding her arms she says sarcastically, "So continue with the history lesson."

Matt sat down on the corner of the blanket and said, "Seth knew I wanted to marry you. He knew I left for Louisiana only to retrieve the shawl my mother made for my future wife. He knew I was to return and he was to tell you I would return in two months time. I never lied to you Greta and before you say a word talk to Doc. He knows . . . just talk to him. Please. I never lied to you . . . I could not do that."

Greta was in shock and outraged as she thought back to that time when Seth convinced her Matt left for good. Then she sunk back down against the tree saying, "Just leave me be Matt . . . please . . . go."

"Matt stands up saying, "Please talk to Doc . . . I am not lying to you."

As Matt walks away, Greta is thinking of what he said and she begins to recap a great many things that she was confused about . . . things Seth would say that did not make much sense or things he did, but at the time she dismissed it without question. She thinks about this quest to push west. Her decision to take the girls west, it was a true and honest decision, more land, a better life for her girls. However, there was something else in this drive to get west that she did not understand. And as usual, this she would dismiss until another time or at least she would try. Right now, she needed to heal, not only her head and leg but her heart also. And . . . confusion is not part of the healing process.

Ellie walked up to Greta carrying a plate with bread and jam on it and a cup of coffee saying, "Here you go. As soon as breakfast is ready I will let Matt know and he will bring you a plate of flapjacks and maple syrup."

"Um . . . no, that will not be necessary. Have one of my girls bring it." She says quietly while looking down at her legs.

Ellie looks strangely at her then says, "Mr. MacGhie asked if we mind that we stay an extra day making it three days rest instead of one. I told him I did not think you would mind."

"I have no problem with that." Greta snapped.

"He was concerned that you may need extra days to rest up since we have been pushing hard."

She spoke impatiently, "Please inform Mr. MacGhie that when he says we leave, we leave and not to worry about what I need. I have no problem leaving or staying any length of time he thinks is necessary."

Ellie looks at Greta strangely and says, "I will let him know that. I am going to check on breakfast and let Matt know how much longer."

Greta's attitude continues, "Do not bother to let Mr. Braummer know unless you plan on feeding him. I said one of my girls can bring me breakfast or you can. And they can help me back to the tent when ready."

Ellie stands up and kind of swings her arms at her sides and says, "Well then. I will do just that. I thought since he brought you out here he was going to spend time with you and. . . "

"That changed."

"Alright. I will let the girls know. Try to rest up and relax. . . "

"I am doing that Ellie . . . see." She waves her hands out over the blanket to emphasize the fact that she was sitting, relaxing, and spilling her coffee.

"Yes Greta. I see. I see a lot!" Ellie says annoyed and turns to leave. Greta realizes how she is sounding and says, "Oh Ellie, I am sorry. I am just hurting. And that is no excuse for my rude behavior to you. If you don't mind I could take some more coffee and will you sit with me for awhile?"

Ellie smiles, "That's more like it. Sure. I will be right back with another cup of coffee and one for me. The girls can handle things."

Ellie approaches the fire, pours two cups of coffee, and says to the girls, "We leave in three days. Take care of what needs to be done. I am going to sit with your mother so let me know when breakfast is ready for her. Then when everything is set up bring your mother back here."

Emma says as she is slicing potatoes, "We will have everything set for her. But I thought Mr. Braummer would bring her back."

"Guess not." Ellie said as she shrugs her shoulders and starts to walk toward Greta.

"Well why not. . . "

"Do not ask. I do not know." Ellie said as she walks away with the cups of coffee. She turned her head long enough to add, "Just let me know when the food is ready."

"Yes Ma'am." Ruth said as she mixes the eggs and flour together for the flapjacks.

Doc walks up saying, "Nice place isn't it. I hear we will be staying three days. Is your coffee ready?"

Claire pours him a cup saying, "Here you go Sir. Ellie told us of the extended stay."

"How is your leg Ruth?"

"Still hard to walk on but I am getting around a lot better. I feel good that I can help Ellie with the cooking and give her a break." Ruth said as she is mixing the flapjacks and heating up the large black fry pan. The butter begins to sizzle as it melts and Ruth mixes the batter faster.

"Katie . . . how is your arm?"

"Still sore Sir. However, I am moving it around a lot more. How is Mother?"

"She is doing as best as can be expected. Mr. Braummer just told me her head was still hurting. I cannot figure out why her head hurts so much. She will enjoy this rest even though she does not think she needs it. You will be setting her in a tent right?"

"Yes Sir that is our plan." Emma said as she drops the potato slices in the other huge blackened fry pan causing a sizzling noise. She grabs the wooden spoon and stirs the potatoes and butter around.

"Good. Now I best get my tent up." Doc leaves and the girls look over at their mother.

Emma says, "After we get the tent up, Claire you help me with Ma. You help too Anne."

"Alright. We will. However, she may not be ready to leave yet. She will be eating as soon as Ruth is done."

"Then we wait for her to call us. But at least we know who will be helping her so stay close to camp." Emma puts a lid over the potatoes as they slowly sizzle to doneness. Ruth dropped spoonfuls of batter onto the melted butter, the aroma of vanilla filled the air as the flapjacks sizzled in the butter. Ruth watched them carefully as not to burn them. When the edges were crispy and many holes appeared on the top of each flapjack Ruth carefully flipped them over showing the golden color of doneness and to complete the other side. As the flapjacks became ready Ruth would put three on a plate and pass the plate to Emma who placed a spoonful of golden fried potatoes along side. Each girl added their own maple syrup. Ellie took two plates and walked back over to where Greta was sitting. Claire carried over their coffee then returned to finish her wonderful breakfast.

When everyone finished eating and the tent put up, Greta called to the girls that she was ready to return. Claire and Emma brought her back to the tent making her feel comfortable. The girls sat around their Mother talking about many things, including Katie, who has been very pleasant and easy to get along with. They compliment her on such.

Katie says nothing and just smiles. Anne and Claire decide to return the blanket to Mr. Braummer while the others continue setting up the inside of the tent.

On the way to Mr. Braummer's tent Claire says, "What is with mother and Mr. Braummer? First, they are nice to each other then they are mad at each other. Do you have any idea Anne?"

"No I do not know. They are both set in their ways. That may be the whole thing . . . ssshhh, Mr. Braummer . . . hello." Anne and Claire wave to him and he returns the wave.

"Hello girls. What brings you to my door step . . . so to speak?" Matt says as he sits on a log near his fire.

"Anne and I came to return the blanket you set out for Mother."

"Oh . . . I see. Well thank you. I would have retrieved it sooner or later." He takes the blanket and tosses it into the tent.

"I guess we should get back now." Claire says.

"See you later girls." He waves to them as they walk away.

"Bye Mr. Braummer."

As the girls wave and walk away, Claire says quietly, "Anne, he and Mother would be good for each other."

"I know. But do not try to convince them of that now."

"I would not dream of it. We best hurry. Emma is setting up another tent."

Emma has most of the second tent set up when the girls arrive to help.

"Hey Emma, looks like you could use a little help." Claire says as she grabs the rope and stakes it to the ground. "I thought we were only putting up one tent.

"I thought two would give us more room if needed. How is Mr. Braummer?"

"Alright I guess. We did not ask him anything about Mother if that is what you are meaning." Claire said.

"Oh I thought for sure you two would."

Anne looks surprised saying, "Why would we? Is it our business?"

"No. But I thought you two were going to make it so."

"Oh I get it Anne. Emma wants us to ask Mr. Braummer about Mother, then we can tell her what we find out and dear Emma does not have to bother Mother with questions. Am I not correct, Emma?"

"Is that true Emma?" Anne said.

"Well . . . he would answer questions from you two a lot easier than if I, Ruth or Ellie questioned him."

"Tie that one Claire, and I do not think I will say a word. I mend clothes not people." Anne says with a smile.

"What about you, Claire?"

"Thanks a lot Emma. You make it sound like I have no choice in the matter." She ties the rope to the stake making it good and tight. Then she stands up quickly and stares out into the night.

Emma seeing her staring says, "Aaaahh, I am sorry. I am just concerned about both of them. I would say it is time for a cup of coffee." Emma goes to the fire where Ellie and Ruth are sitting. Claire and Anne continue to tie off the tent and talk about gathering the blankets to put inside the tent.

"Well Emma. What did they say?" Ellie said anxiously.

"Oh ladies . . . those two are tough. Anne says she mends clothes not people and Claire got upset because to her it sounded like she had no choice in the matter."

"At least the thought was put in their mind. Maybe they will talk to him now about Mother." Ruth said while pouring coffee and adding a drop of whiskey like Mrs. Sarah O'Hara did back home. "I will make some spice cake and send it over with the girls. That just might open up a conversation. What do you think?"

"It might work Ruth. Do not do it right away. They are not dumb you know." Emma said as Ruth hands her the whiskey coffee.

"I know. Maybe in the morning I will make it." Ruth said as she takes a sip of her whiskey coffee.

"That sounds better. Thanks for the Mrs. O'Hara cup of coffee. We have not had any whiskey on this trip and it does taste good." Emma said as Ellie agrees and they all enjoy the tasty coffee.

Claire and Anne walk up hearing part of the conversation and they question, "Do not do what right now and what is Mrs. O'Hara's cup of coffee?"

Ruth ignores the questions of the two girls and says, "What do you think about Katie?" At the same time Marie, Alex and Isaac walk up.

Alex says, "What about Katie?"

Ruth and Emma continue in their conversation not hearing the others question.

"I am not sure Ruth. Something is different about her. She has not complained once since the attack and has become nice. Here she comes."

Claire was looking at them waiting for some sort of answer. When she figures none will be given she says, "Fine . . . do not answer the questions. We do not need any answers to your silly conversation." She then sat down looking at Marie, Alex, and Isaac who sit down wondering what Claire meant. They are given cups of whiskey coffee and enjoy it while still wondering about the conversation that was not clarified.

"Hello everyone, please hand me a cup of coffee?" Katie said standing with a smile.

"That is it. I cannot take it any more Katherine Jean Yancey! What is wrong with you? We all want to know. And we want to know right now!" Emma said as she looked at her and then the others and back at Katie.

"Well Emma. Are you referring to my not complaining about everything?" she says smiling.

"Yes! You are actually nice. What is with that?" Emma says as she hands her a cup of coffee.

Katie sits down saying, "I got shot in the arm by an arrow. Ruth, you were shot in the leg by an arrow. Mother was shot in the leg by an arrow that broke her bone and she was almost scalped and killed by that Indian. I figure my complaining would be more troublesome to everyone. So I decided not to complain."

"Just like that, you decided not to complain. Are you fooling? Is this how you will be all the time? From now on?" Emma smiles and looks at the others sitting around drinking the Mrs. O'Hara coffee and actually enjoying the new Katie.

Katie smiles back and says, "I have been writing everything down in my journal and when the time is right the old Katie will return and you can count on that!"

They all look at Katie in shock and Ellie says, "Katie . . . do you mean to tell us that you are going back to your awful whinny attitude . . . after being so nice? You cannot do that Katie! Do you know how pleasant you are? You are such a joy to be around. You must be joshing with us."

"No Ma'am. I am not joshing about anything and I do not care what you or anyone else thinks. You do not realize how difficult this has been for me and I would not be so nice if it was not for my journal. I can write it all down. . . ."

"Yes Katie . . . write it all down and stay nice." Ellie encourages.

"No thank you. That is not my plan. I am going to go lay down for a while. See you all later."

They all watch Katie walk away and Emma says, "I am so angry right now I could give her a good switching!"

"No." Ruth says, "Wait until she is back to not liking things and complaining . . . it will be easier to break a switch on her behind."

Everyone laughs but then quiets down and thinks of what an awful thing she is going to do. They then turn their attention to watch the rest of the camp being set up. They see Doc walk over to Mr. Braummer's tent and hope he can find out what is going on and maybe Doc will fill them in later.

Doc walks up to Matt questioning why he is here and not with Greta. Matt tells him what happened when he was with her. . .

"Well Matt. Maybe you just have to give it time . . . give her space. . . "

"What! Time . . . space . . . oh come on Doc! There is more to this than even I know!"

"Listen . . . she has been through a great deal and I have to check her out anyway. If she asks me anything you know I will tell her the truth." Doc says as he pats Matt on the back.

Doc walks away and Matt thinks . . . 'Do not worry . . . oh sure . . . Greta is the one I did not think I had to worry about. I thought we were good. Now I have Greta and Emily to worry about. . . Emily . . . she should have gotten my letter by now . . . time . . . space . . . as if there is not enough around here!' He sits down looking at the space around him then lays down looking at the sky . . . he thinks . . . 'more space.'

CHAPTER TWO

Emily stood firm with folded arms on the large front porch of her huge two story home. Minton stood quietly behind one of the opened double white doors listening to the orders barked by the fat man sitting on his restless horse. Emily glared at the fat man's stone face as she listened to him then she spoke, "Mr. Hadley. I thought I made myself very clear to you and your son Owen on numerous occasions that I have no desire to marry him. My brother was here on one such occasion. Why would you think anything has changed?"

"Again, I repeat myself so you will understand! You, Miss Emily, will marry Owen before you are too old to birth my grandsons. Owen will take his proper title as Master of Whispering Oaks and all the slaves will obey him!"

"Excuse me Sir . . . but you have forgotten one piece of valued information. Mr. Matthew Braummer, my brother, owns Whispering Oaks. Not I. Therefore, leaving your son, Owen, Master of nothing! Including me!" Emily smiles.

"You are very wrong dear lady. My information is clear!"

"Your information, Sir, is no clearer than the morning fog! I wish you to leave the property of Mr. Matthew Braummer at once and make note that you and your son are no longer welcome on this property called Whispering Oaks! Good bye Mr. Hadley!"

As Emily turns to enter her home Hadley is driven to a higher rage, yelling, "Nobody speaks that way to me!" He pulls the whip from the side of his saddle and lays a severe mark across the back of Emily ripping her dress and tearing into the soft flesh as she screams out in agony and unbelief that he would do such a thing. He lays another whiplash against her back and she falls against the side of the opened door gripping the wood and feeling for the handle, as another stripe is laid on her back. Tears fall from her eyes, her face hard against the wood door as she leans against the door gripping the handle and begins to straightening herself up as best she could. Emily turns her face to Hadley, in agony, her eyes meet his and she says, "Your have forgotten Sir, my brother, Mr. Matthew Braummer owns Whispering Oaks . . . (she pauses for a moment and continues). . . Not I! Leaving your son Owen master of nothing . . . including me! Now leave!" She continues to stair into his eyes. Hadley lays a forth stripe across her back pushing her hard into the door and shouts "You will marry Owen and he will be Master of Whispering Oaks! Mark my words or prepare for another lashing Miss Emily Braummer!" he then lays a fifth stripe across her back as she slowly attempts to pull the door, Hadley, glaring at her, turns his horse and gallops away screaming loudly, "Owen will be Master of Whispering Oaks, and your slaves will bow to him!" As Emily is falling into the house, she is pulling the door closed, she does not want Hadley to see any weakness. As Emily falls to the floor, a letter falls out of her pocket and Minton is there to catch her before she hits the floor.

Minton, holding the limp body of Emily now covered in blood, picks up the letter, and shouts for others to come help. They help Minton carry Emily to the kitchen where they lay her on the table to tend to her wounds. Minton gives instructions to the others as she tucks the letter in her apron pocket, retrieves a pan and thinks out loud, "Who cane I git to read dis hare letter? Who I gonna trust? Oh Masta Matthew gonna be mad. Oh Lord, who cane I git? I noze . . . Miss Lilly. She I cane trust." With that she says, "Zoe . . . go fetch Miss Lilly right quick . . . move child! Run like da lightenin'!" Minton now concentrates on slowly removing pieces of material from the deep lashes in the skin. She then begins to speak out loud again, "Oh Miss Emily, how he do dis to you? He crazy man! Dat man, he so mean! Somebody needs to take 'n' whip him like he do poor Miss Emily. Oh dis is bad . . . Miss Emily . . . If I waz white man I noz what I do to dat bad fat man 'n' ropen iz too good for him!"

Able came running in, "Minton, dat Mr. Hadely say he comin' back for her in da mornin' and he gonna make Miss Emily marry his son, Mr. Owen!"

"Oh no, no, no, we gots to git Miss Emily away from here. But how we gonna do dat?" she says as she continues to remove pieces of blood torn cloth from Emily's back.

Able says smiling, "I noz, we cane hide her wif our people. Nobody find her, no body!"

Minton stops what she was doing and looks strangely at Able saying, "You dumb man! How dis here white girl gonna blend in wif our people? Sometime I think you got no brains! God just forgot to give you brains! Dumb man! Now git out! I got serious work to do here!"

Able starts to walk away saying, "Doan be callin' me no dumb man! Iz know what Iz talkin' 'bout. I noz we cane hide her!'

"Hush up your mouth and git out ta here! Let me workn 'n' think . . . now go!"

"Miss Lilly is here 'n' da dumb man is goin' out da door." As Able leaves, he bows to Minton who gives him a mean look and shoos him with her hands.

Miss Lilly stops in her steps, grabbing her face, as she is horrified to see Emily's bloody back saying, "Oh heavens, what has happened here? Dear, dear Emily, who has done this awful thing to you?" She studies her back then begins to help Minton remove more pieces of clothing that is imbedded in the skin. Minton and Zoe tell her what happened.

"Oh that Mr. Hadley is a mean and awful man! How could he do such a thing like this? Oh Emily, Emily!"

"Miss Lilly, dis here letter fell from Miss Emily's pocket. Cane you read it? I tink it from Master Matthew."

"Let me see it." Lilly looks at the letter and gets excited as she reads . . . then she begins to read it out loud to Minton and Zoe;

{My Dearest Sister Emily, It is finally going to happen sister, and this is true, I am going to marry Mrs. Greta Yancey. Nevertheless, in order to do that I must find her as she is somewhere between Earleysburg and the far western country. By the time you get this I should be near San Louie on the Mississippi River. Do you remember me talking about Doctor William Allen? He will be traveling with me as he is in pursuit of one Mrs. Ellie Cooper. She is the one that once owned the Boarding House in Earleysburg. Dear Sister I am confused, not knowing where to find her. Though I have sent word to Mrs. Coopers Son, Tom, the Mountain Man/Trapper, I am still perplexed as to where these women could possibly be. Oh yes and Mrs. Yancey has her seven daughters along on this journey. You know I have always loved her and I want to make her my wife for as long as we both live. It is most regrettable that I will not be able to come visit you this year. However, rest assured that when I do come I will be a married man and bringing my wife. Please make known to Minton and Able that I will miss them. Until my next letter, your loving Brother, Matthew.}

"So, Mr. Matthew is heading to San Louie and in pursuit of one Mrs. Greta Yancey whom he plans to marry! This is wonderful news! Do you know if Emily read the letter?"

"No Ma'am, I dont know if she read da letter. But Ma'am, how we gon git him? What we do wif Miss Emily? Mr. Hadley gon take her in da mornin'!"

"Oh no, Minton. He will not take her from her home! I will see to that! Zoe, please get my husband and brothers at once!"

"Yes Ma'am." Zoe was off again.

"We will just see how Mr. Hadley deals with my husband and brothers. Minton, I will go to her room and prepare it for her. I will then return with her robe."

"No Miss Lilly, no robe. We gon wrap her loose in dis here cloth . . . then no cloth on wounds . . . she be more of comfort in bed." Minton says as she holds up a cotton cloth.

"Yes, yes that is good. You are doing a fine job Minton and I thank you for Miss Emily." Lilly gives Minton a hug.

"Oh Miss Lilly, thank you but we do anything for Miss Emily. She so good to us, we just gots to help her. We just gots to."

"Yes I know. You all are very loyal to the Braummer family." Lilly pats Minton on her back saying, "We are helping her and more help is on the way." She then leaves to prepare the bedroom.

In no time, Emily is resting in her bed with Minton and Lilly at her side. Zoë returns with Lilly's husband, Alistair and her brothers, Clint and Edward. As they enter the kitchen, their eyes fall upon the ripped, blood-filled dress lying on the floor and understanding hits hard. . . . Mr. Hadley has to be stopped! They question where Lilly is and Wenna tells them. The men bolt for the stairs and straight up to her room. Alistair was first to enter the room. The horrified look on his face was enough to say how awful the whip marks were. The men all stood in shock to think another man would do this to another human, let alone a lady. Neither Matt's family nor Alistair's family practiced this behavior and Mr. Hadley had now created an anger that was beyond words.

With tightened fists at his side Alistair said, "Where is Matthew?"

Lilly shows him the letter.

"Why could he not be where we could get to him easily? Zoë have the boys put our horses in the barn. It looks like we will be here for awhile."

"Yes Sa. I do dat."

Minton speaks, "Sir we gots to git her out a here. Mr. Hadley comin' in da mornin' to fetch her an' make her marry his son Mr. Owen."

"Do not fret none at all. That will not happen. Could you have one of the girls make us some coffee?"

"Yes Sir." Minton goes to the top of the stairs and seeing Wenna tells her to fix coffee for the men.

"We need to make some hard decisions."

Lilly stood up saying, "Not in here. You all go down to the dining hall and let Emily rest." As she is speaking this she is pushing the men out of the room.

The men leave and Lilly sits back down on a chair next to the bed cooling Emily's face and watching for any signs that she will wake up.

In the dining hall, two close neighbors who heard the disturbing news greet Alistair, Clint, and Edward. As they sit around the huge table having coffee and discuss this old plantation of the Braummer Family, Whispering Oaks, and why Mr. Hadley is so interested in it. This plantation of the Bruammers yields a great abundance of cotton, cattle, some sugar cane, and timber on the 10,000 acres. They discuss the reputation of Whispering Oaks that has always been the care of the slaves and animals. Slaves that were not treated badly and are respected for the work they do and have done. The family worked side by side with slaves in the beginning to build this marvelous plantation into a prosperous business for all. To the Braummer family, this sounded like the right thing to do. Especially since they could not have built such an empire had it not been for the slaves. Other landowners felt the same and treated their slaves with respect. Others did not. They discuss the fact that Minton and Abel took over where their very own parents left off; marring spouses from this very plantation and raising a family to continue the work set forth by their parents. They became main top servants . . . in House Servants. . . Minton was the main cook and Able's wife gave the orders to the other girls that worked in the house. Able was their main manservant; working side by side with Minton's husband handling all work outside. They were there when the Braummer's eight children were born and they helped bury six of the children . . . Matthew, being the eldest at age 28 was away when his four brothers and two sisters were killed. Emily then was left to find her way home and tell of the happenings. She was thirteen at the time. Emily could never identify who did the awful killings because her sisters hid her when they saw the strange men approaching. As the years went on Matthew would travel more and when his parents passed on he told Emily the plantation was hers. Although she could not show ownership on paper . . . it was still hers. Matthew bought the tavern in Earleysburg and visited his sister as much as possible. The discussion then turned to how to contact Matthew and inform him of Emily. Edward and Clint offer to leave at first light to find him. The others would stand firm and not let anything happen to Emily, the land or her slaves.

CHAPTER THREE

"Tomorrow we leave girls. Make sure you get to bed early for a good night's rest. Four in the morning is mighty early." Ellie said as she stirs the pot of bubbling venison stew for supper. "How is your spice cake Ruth? Mr. Braummer has been waiting for some."

"It is done. I made it earlier today. Anne, would you please take this over to Mr. Braummer. I am going to take mother her dinner as soon as it is done."

"Alright, do you want to come with me Claire?" Anne said as she takes the spice cake.

"Yes, I will walk over with you."

As they are leaving, Ruth glances a smile at Emma and Ellie who also smile back.

As the girls walk they look around at the prairie land and small bluffs that surround them. The girls reach the tent saying, "Hello Mr. Braummer."

"Hello Claire, Anne. What have you there?" Mr. Braummer says as he climbs out of the tent. Claire hands the cake to Mr. Braummer smiling and saying, "It is the spice cake Ruth made. We heard you have been waiting for it."

"Yes I have. Thank you. Please sit with me. I just made fresh coffee and we can all enjoy some with this wonderful cake. Here let me get a blanket to lie on the ground." He hands the cake to Claire and spreads out a blanket then he grabs some cups and plates. Claire puts the cake down on a stump near them saying, "Alright, since we do not have anything to do anyway." They then sat down by the fire. Matt fills the cups with coffee and hands them to the girls. He then sits down cutting the spice cake and hands them to the girls.

Anne says, "Oh thank you Sir. However, this was all for you. The coffee is enough."

"Have it anyway. This way your sister will have to make more."

They smile and sit silence for a while eating and drinking coffee. The girls look at his tent set up and notice how neat everything was. Then Matt clears his throat and breaks the silence saying, "I remember the first time I had this cake . . . only it was not as mild as this one. Remember?"

The girls laugh then Claire says, "Do we ever remember. Ruth had almost everyone feeling extremely happy."

"Yes and all the men kept eating it and eating it. They could not get enough of it." Anne said laughing.

"Well, hel . . . Oh I mean, well no, that rum sure was good in it."

They laugh again and Claire says, "It was actually whiskey Ruth put on the cake, not rum."

And they all laugh then silence.

Again, Matt breaks the quietness saying, "I remember the last time I had it too."

Claire spoke, "That night before we left, right?"

"Yes." He said with a smile.

Claire continues, "It was a fine night right Anne?"

"Oh it sure was. I never danced so much in all my life. My legs were actually sore."

"Yes, girls, so where mine!" said Matt as he laughed and rubbed his legs.

"Of course they would be Mr. Braummer. I will tell you a secret. . . Mother's legs were very sore also."

"No . . . you don't say."

"Yes Sir! You just wore Mother out. Right Claire?"

"Even though, she was still having fun wasn't she?" Matt asked.

"Oh Mr. Braummer . . . she talked about that night for weeks after. How much fun she had and the shawl you gave her. Sir, she loves it. Right Claire?"

"Yes she does and she wears it every chance she gets . . . even now when resting in the wagon, she has it with her." Claire said as she takes a sip of coffee smiling.

"She does? Well I am confused now."

"About what Sir?" Claire questions looking with a frown.

"About your Mother . . . you know I love her don't you?"

The girls smile and nod their heads quickly.

"I thought she loved me."

"Oh I am sure she does Sir." Claire says as Anne kicks her foot.

"Then what is the problem?"

The girls look at each other and Matt continues before they can say anything.

"If it was not for this quest of getting you girls west, which is so much a part of her life now and yet there seems to be something else that I cannot quite put my finger on. Know what I mean?"

"Yes Sir we do. But Sir . . . do not be confused."

"No? Well I am. I cannot help it. I am very confused!" Matt says as he refills his cup.

"Sir, it is like Anne said, do not be. Remember Preacher Anderson talking about confusion?"

"No can't say that I have." He fills the girl's cups with coffee.

"Thank you for the coffee. Confusion is not from God. In confusion, Preacher Anderson says, you begin to doubt Gods Word and that is what the devil wants . . . to keep us confused then we cannot do what God wants us to do because we are not listening to God, we are listening to the devils lies."

"I do not know what to do. I came out here in hopes of marrying your mother, but she keeps pushing me away."

"Mr. Braummer where is your Bible?"

"In my tent . . . I will get it." He gets up and returns with his Bible giving it to Claire. "Here you go."

"Thank you. The scripture in First Corinthians 14:33 says, in the first part, 'God is not the author of confusion, but of peace. . . ' Preacher Anderson said confusion means instability, disorder, unstable."

"I sure missed that sermon. So how are we supposed to act when confusion comes in?" Matt says scratching his head.

"Well Sir . . . Preacher Anderson said the opposite of disorder is order, the opposite of instability is being stable. He said since God is a God of peace then we ask Him for peace. It says in James 1:8 'a double minded man is unstable in all his ways.' Unstable and confusion go hand in hand."

"Then what do I do?" Matt said gripping his cup and shaking his head.

"Well Mr. Braummer . . . I just ask God to take my confusion and replace it with His wisdom that He gives freely to those who ask. I then ask for His peace. Then work hard at pushing the wrong thinking out of my thinking. Preacher Anderson said it is definitely a battle but the battle is in the mind."

Claire added, "That is why we wear the Armor of God . . . for battle."

"Yes, yes . . . I agree with both of you and I do remember reading about the Armor of God. It is in Ephesians chapter six. I also remember that when I read that I noticed there was no armor for the backside to wear. So I guess that means we do not turn and run." Matt smiles an assuring smile.

Slapping her knee Claire says, "That is right. We face the problem head on and put all our trust in Jesus."

Anne added, "Maybe reading more of the Bible will help you. It sure helps Ma and Emma."

"Well I gotta admit, you are right about that. Preacher Anderson gave that Bible to me. Time to put it to good use, thank you." He said as Claire returns the Bible to his hands.

"Thank you, Sir, for the cake and coffee. We best be getting back now." Anne said as both girls stand up to leave.

Smiling he says, "Thank you both very much." Looking at the Bible he continues, "I do have reading at that. Preacher Anderson did give me his very own Bible and I am sure it was not for packing space."

They all laugh as the girls leave. Matt takes the Bible and lantern into his tent, sets it down then retrieves his coffee and a large piece of spice cake. He sits down on the blanket and picks up the Bible, opens it to read a note from Preacher Anderson.

'Took ye long 'nough. God is patient. He is waiting to listen to what ye have to say . . . now sit in His lap and talk to yer Father who loves ye.'

"Here goes. James chapter one, verse one. . . . *'James, a servant of God and of the Lord Jesus Christ, to the twelve tribes which are scattered abroad, greeting.* Verse two . . . *My brethren, count it all joy when ye fall into divers temptations;'* Matt stops and comments, "Joy in temptation? Oh yea how is that done? I know I know, keep reading . . . *'knowing this that the trying of your faith worketh patience. . .'*" Matt continues reading and finds he has been reading for hours when Doc comes by.

"Hey in the tent! Matt! You sleeping with your light on?" He pulls the flap back and sees Matt reading. "Oh I am sorry Matt; I did not mean to disturb you."

Rubbing his eyes saying, "No Doc that is alright. What brings you by? Anything wrong"

"No nothings wrong. Your fire went out and . . . have you even eaten dinner? It is late you know. We have to be up at four in the morning." Doc said very concerned.

"Yes I ate dinner and spice cake too. Had a wonderful talk with Claire and Anne and just enjoyed some very good reading. Of course I know we have to be up at four

and if you are so concerned why are you not sleeping?"
Matt said.

"Well . . . it is not that late. Hey Matt, I did disturb you.
I am sorry. I will leave you be."

"No Doc. No, need to. Here I will build up the fire and
heat the coffee. I could use one."

At that, Matt marked where he was in the Bible,
crawled out of his tent and while building up the fire to
heat the coffee they talked.

"You know Doc. Those two girls of Greta are very special. Lot of wisdom in their young minds. Did you know
confusion does not come from God?"

Doc looks at him strangely then says, "Oh yes . . . I remember Preacher Anderson talking about that."

With the coffee hot, they sit and discuss many things
until Mr. MacGhie comes along to tell them they best turn
in along with everyone else. Mr. MacGhie checks the ones
on watch as he rides around the camp in the quiet of the
night. Stars twinkling against a black sky, a few cattle
noises, and then all is silent. He stops on a small bluff and
looks over the somber area thinking 'All is well, the camp
is now quiet.'

CHAPTER FOUR

Just before dawn crept over Whispering Oaks, Edward and Clint, Lilly's brothers, tie down the packs on one mule, saddle their horses, and prepare to leave.

You have what you need boys?" Alistair questions.

"Yes. Once we get to San Louie, we will begin to inquire of Matthew. Alistair, be careful. You know Hadley is no man to fool with." Edward said as he mounts his horse.

"Nor am I." Alistair said looking back at the house to see Lilly in a pink robe watching from the kitchen door he continues, "Mr. Hadley has gone too far. I have tolerated him long enough . . . we all have. He needs to be stopped!"

"Yes I realize that. Just do not do anything you will regret Alistair. Let Matthew handle this situation." Clint says as he adjusts himself on his horse.

"Until you find him and until he handles it what do you propose I do? Just sit back and wait. Mark my word brothers, if Hadley forces the issue he will be met with great opposition. Now off with you. Your travel is long and hard."

"Pray we find him quickly."

Alistair watches as Edward and Clint leave. He then returns to the house saying to Lilly, "Stay away from all windows and doors. Only we men will be seen and Minton this includes you and the girls."

"Yes Sa." Minton says and returns to the kitchen to inform the others.

"Do you truly expect trouble dear Alistair?"

"Lilly, with a man like Mr. Hadley always expect trouble."

The men took their places at the windows. Alistair sits on the porch unarmed waiting for Hadley. As the sun begins to rise, a large group of men on horseback are seen approaching the home of Emily Braummer.

"Alistair! Hello! We heard Miss Emily is in need of help and we are here to give help!"

"Thank you Mr. Howard. Have the men ride to the barn and enter the back of the house. My brothers are there also. They can tell you more of what has transpired here."

Behind Mr. Trevor Howard set every plantation owner, big and small, of the surrounding areas with their Sons and Son-in-laws.

"Yes Sir. Go now men, do as Mr. Duvos says. Have you a plan?"

"I do not want a war. What he did to Miss Braummer could very well cause a war. I trust God will have to do the guiding on this one." Alistair said lighting his thin cigar.

"Where do you want me?"

"I think each head of the plantation should sit on the porch. The rest of the men in the house stationed at windows."

"Very good, I will instruct them." At that, Mr. Howard rides to the barns to inform the others what the plan is. Soon about twenty-two men join Alistair on the porch all armed and waiting. Proud southern gentlemen sit ready to give defense and protect the land of their friend, while other proud southern gentlemen take their stance in the home of their friend, fully armed and ready for anything.

"Alistair. You do realize we are no match for Hadley's armed men." Trevor said taking his seat.

"Not so my friend, look on the floor in front of you. Pistols, loaded, lay waiting to be used if necessary. When your pistols are empty just drop and continue to shoot."

"Wonderful thinking." Trevor smiles nodding his head in agreement.

"Yes . . . though I pray we need not use them." Alistair said as he looked down the path.

The men all agree and wait.

Just before noon, riders are seen coming up the roadway to the house.

"Well . . . what have we here? A meeting of owners? Tell Miss Emily Braummer this carriage behind me is for her. I will wait."

Alistair sits calmly saying, "No Sir. Miss Braummer will not be getting into that carriage and you will be leaving this plantation now!"

Shouting at Alistair, "Who are you to tell me to get off this plantation? It will soon be owned by me!"

"Leave Hadley. We want no bloodshed." Trevor Howard spoke.

"You sit there so smug thinking I will listen. While you're very homes are being raided by my men at this exact time. I am no fool!" Hadley said as his horse moves about in an unsettled manner.

"If true . . . Hadley . . . they will be met with great opposition. We do not leave our homes unprotected!" says Trevor Howard.

Hadley shouts, "Emily Braummer get out here now! I told you I would be back for you!"

"You are wasting your breath. She will not be coming out."

"You cannot stop her!" Hadley shouts.

"No. We can stop you. By her choice." Alistair said as he continued with the other men to hold their places on the porch and in their chairs.

Hadley pulls his pistol and aims it at Alistair saying, "I could kill you right now . . . each one of you fools sitting there."

"You may think you can." Alistair waves his arm and his brothers and Lilly's three other brothers come out of the house with rifles aimed at Hadley and his men. More men came from the side of the home and on the balcony, all aiming rifles at the horsemen. "You need to leave Hadley and trust me . . . this home will be well protected from here on out."

Hadley yells, "I am not done with any of you! You will pay for this! Be forewarned! You will pay!" He turns his horse and leaves with his men following.

Alistair turns to the others saying, "This will not be easy but we must protect Whispering Oaks. If he wins . . . who will be next? Go now and see to your families needs then send one from each of your homes to stay here. We will work out a rotation schedule later. I thank you all for your support and help for Miss Braummer."

"We are proud to help out. In helping Miss Braummer we are helping our own homes." said Trevor Howard. They leave to find their homes in safe order and no bloodshed needed to be spilled. Soon one man from each plantation arrived to help protect Whispering Oaks and Miss Emily.

CHAPTER FIVE

Mr. MacGhie guided the travelers onward to Cantonment Leavenworth where they enter the great prairie. Great caution was taken as they traveled through Indian country. This is where the Indians were assigned land by the government. It was a dangerous area since this is not where the Indians want to be. The girls paid close attention to what the men of their camp instructed. The soldiers accompanied them through certain areas. Rain was heavy and the crossing of rivers severe. The rain made it harder for travel. The smaller wagon belonging to Isaac and Alex would sink deep in the soft watery mud on numerous occasions. While the heavy rain continued to pour down it took a lot of effort on the horses working hard to get a grip, and the men as they tried to get a foothold in mud that would suck the boots in place not wanting to let go. They pushed and pulled to get the wheels moving. The men often lost their foothold and fell into the mud only to get up and try again. Finally, after fighting this gushy mud, the men won and the wagon was on a roll again. They beat the thick prairie mud once again that wanted to hold their captives forever.

"Will it ever stop raining?" Claire said as she helps set up camp. "Up until that area just past Liberty we had good weather then the land opens up and the sky pours out the rain. And if I have to lead one more horse through the mud . . . well, I do not know what I will do, but, I will do something!"

"I am sure it will pass." Ellie said while putting up the cook tent. The girls were dripping wet and hurried to help Ellie so she could start a fire and they all could be dry again. As they help Ellie she continues talking, "You are not the only one leading horses through the mud. Think of this, without all those men over there we would be attempting to turn wheels, dig and push wagons which I do not think we could have accomplished. Only one wagon keeps getting stuck, Isaac's. Because the wheels are narrower than the bigger wagons."

"You are right about that. And we would be stuck in Indian Territory. I know this rain will pass. We will have more rivers to cross that the rain has made traitorous before we get to . . . what did they call it . . . Cantonment Leavenworth." Claire said as she wiped raindrops from her face.

"Yes and we are traveling with experienced men that I am very grateful for all their help and knowledge."

"I am too. I am thinking of Alex and her fear of river crossings. Those rivers ahead of us may not be very nice you know." Claire said as she looks ahead then continues with the work at hand.

Emma walks up trying to tuck her wet hair under her wet hat saying, "Do not worry about her, Claire. Isaac has her handled quite well. Think of it, she has crossed the past many rivers with no problem. I do not think we need to worry about her anymore. She is in good hands."

"Yes I suppose you are right." Remarks Claire as she ties the end of the rope to a stake in the ground.

"Emma, give me a hand with the stove will you please? Soon we will be dry. Do not worry about Alex, Claire. She is doing just fine. What you need to keep in mind is what they said about the Indians around here. Apparently, they are not too friendly since our Government assigned them to this area. Like Mr. MacGhie said, this area is theirs right now and we are the trespassers . . . with somewhat permission. Of course this permission is from our Government, might not be from the Indians." Ellie says as she unhitches the back of a wagon.

"Which is why we are to be extra careful right?" Emma said.

"Right."

The stove was moved in the ten, filled with wood and soon the warmth of the fire began to fill the tent.

"Oh that does feel good." Greta said while Anne and Claire help her in and set her on a cot.

"We are sorry Ma that you got wet. We did not see that hole we lead you in." Anne said with Claire agreeing.

"I must say the cold water and mud certainly wakes a body up right quick. Do not worry. No harm has been done. I will change and be warm in to time." Greta says as she is removing her blouse and Claire removes her shoes and socks then skirt. She wraps her in a quilt and tucks it around her until the room is warm enough for her to put on dry clothing.

"Yes and soon tea to warm us all. It is almost done." Ellie said trying not to laugh.

The girls brought in dry clothing and more quilts for each of them. They strung some rope across the tent to hang the wet clothing in one area to dry. Soon they were all sitting and enjoying the tea. And Greta felt better after getting into dry clothing.

"Hello in the tent." Doc sticks his head in the tent continuing, "I heard riders coming in from the north saying there was clear weather ahead of us."

"Thank you Doc. Come in and warm yourself. Emma run and get more blankets please." Greta says smiling.

"Thank you Greta, I will do just that. How are you doing?"

"Better each day. I actually feel stronger . . . even in this weather."

"You are looking healthier. I also stopped by to inform you of Indians visiting. Do not be alarmed but do stay in your tent. Mr. MacGhie says they usually visit with the men then leave. So stay put! MacGhie said we will be in Cantonment Leavenworth tomorrow morning."

"Good and we will stay put. You do not have to tell us twice." Ellie says while pouring a cup of tea for Doc. Emma and Ruth enter in with dry blankets and question the 'stay put' talk as Ellie hands Doc a cup of tea and pours more for the others while Doc explains the situation to the rest of the girls.

Marie questions, "What tribe would they be?"

The answer came from outside the tent, "Maybe Delaware, Kickapoo. Kanzas very close." Tom and Brave Eagle enter in smiling. Brave Eagle gave the answer. Tom says, "Regardless of the tribe . . . stay put!"

"We will. Would you like some tea?" Emma asks.

"Yes and then we must go."

The men sit down on a blanket with the rest of the ladies and talk about this meeting of the Indians. It is explained that they meet to mainly exchange gifts. Tom thinks it is to see the strength of the group and Brave Eagle agreed which is why the women must stay in their tents. With the evening getting on, the men leave to prepare for their guests.

Greta says, "This is a good night for some scripture reading. What do you think Emma?"

"Yes it is but I . . ."

Just then, the flap opens and Doc says, "Yes you forgot these so I retrieved them for you. I could only grab three . . . will that be enough?"

"Yes. Thank you for thinking about our Bibles." Emma said smiling.

"Good night." Doc leaves closing the flap. "And tie this flap tight!"

"Yes Sir, he certainly does not want us to leave does he?" Ellie said as she pulls out some bread and jam.

Doc's voice is heard, "That is exactly right ladies. Stay put!"

The girls laugh and say good night again to Doc. Ellie and Claire spreads jam on bread handing a slice to each girl. Anne pours more tea in the cups of the girls and Emma opens to the scripture, Galatians 1:6 and says, "I will continue where I left off . . . it reads, *'I marvel that ye are so soon removed from him that called you into the grace of Christ unto another gospel. Which is not another; but there be some that trouble you, and would pervert the gospel of Christ. But though we, or an angel from heaven, preach any other gospel unto you than that which we have preached unto you, let him be accursed. As we said before, so say I now, if any man preach any other gospel unto you that ye have received, let him be accursed. For do I now persuade men, or God? Or do I seek to please men? For if I pleased men, I should not be a servant of Christ.'*

Marie interrupts as she is fixing a place for her to lie down, "Emma does God hate anything?"

"Why would you ask that?"

"Oh I heard some men talking and well . . . does he?"

"As a matter of fact he does . . . in Proverbs 6:16 it reads, *'These six things doth the Lord hate, yes, seven are an abomination unto him: a proud look, a lying tongue, and hands that shed innocent blood, a heart that deviseth wicked imaginations, feet that be swift in running to mischief, a false witness that speaks lies and he that soweth discord among brethren.'* Does that answer your question Marie?"

"It sure does. Thank you." Marie says as she eats some warm bread and finishes her tea along with the others.

Emma continues, "I have one more scripture to read then we can all get to sleep. In Psalms, chapter ninety verse seventeen it reads, *'And let the beauty of the Lord our God be upon us: and establish thou the work of our hands upon us; yea, the work of our hands establish thou it.'* Now my dear sister's give thanks to God for all that we have and sleep well. Good night."

All return good nights, and lie listening to the rain on the tent and the distant voices of men talking and laughing and the girls give thanks to God and fall asleep.

CHAPTER SIX

San Louie—

"Edward. What was the name of that Trapper we were to find?"

"Mr. Paarday at the Den Trading Post."

"There it is." Edward points ahead of them to a log building of considerable size. The men dismount and tie their horses and mule to the hitching post and enter in. Looking around they see a lot of fur piled high along with an array of supplies stockpiled for the traveler and mountain men. As they look around, they see a small stout Frenchman carrying a gunpowder barrel.

"Good day Sir. Are you Paarday?" Clint questions.

"Wee, I am Paarday. Who inquires of me?" He looks at the tall men in buckskin attire.

"I am Edward and this is my brother Clint. We were told you know the whereabouts of a one Mr. Matthew Braummer."

"Dat could vaaree well be. May I first ask why Monsieur, is it you seek de one Mr. Mat'ew Braummer?"

"Yes of course. We must find Mr. Braummer and take him back home. His sister is in need of his immediate help." Edward said.

"Aaahh. I cain only say de direction day go in. Along de Missouri to Cantonment Leavenworth den to Fort William. Day be 'bout tree week ahead of you eef all went well."

"Three weeks! That is not good Clint."

"Oh sure . . . is good. Day travel slow wit wagons and fur companee. You see . . . you catch dem in no time."

"What say we start out early in the morning?"

"Yes Edward that would be good."

44

Paarday tells them of a good place near by to stay for the night. Clint and Edward stock up before heading out. The men mounted their horses and head to the Brimley Tavern where they enjoyed a wonderful hot meal and comfortable beds. Come morning they repacked the mule and stopped to thank Paarday for his hospitality.

"If we push hard Edward we can close the distance."

"Only stopping when necessary." Clint said as he mounted his horse and grabbed the rope of their mule.

"Yes." Edward also mounted his horse and waved to Paarday as they turned their horses west.

They push onward in their quest to find Matthew Braummer. In their traveling, they hear of the wagons that were attacked by the Prairie Banditos and the brave women that stood them off with some men from a Fur Company. Clint and Edward took extra care to help keep alert and sharp to their unknown surroundings. Arriving at Liberty, they hear the commotion going on about the Mormons and leave after getting supplies. They now travel to Cantonment Leavenworth in hopes of catching up with Matthew Braummer.

CHAPTER SEVEN

As the group approached Cantonment Leavenworth, they look at the Missouri River, in an unexpected sudden bend, it rushes with fantastic swiftness against a rock-bound shore; from here the ground rises with a bold sweep to a hundred feet or more, then sloping gently into a shallow vale, it rises equally again, and thus a number of hills are formed. The group crosses by ferry. When they reach the top of the hill the girls are in awe with this different land. Every line of every surface is curved with symmetry and beauty. On these hill-tops, shaded by forest trees stood Cantonment Leavenworth.

"Oh Emma, do you see how far the Missouri River goes?"

"Yes and when you think it ended you look further through the majestic forests and by those massive bluffs and there it is again. Looks like it is going right into the sky." Ruth continued, "And look there, on the other side the rolling prairies, with groves and west that grassy ridge! Look how vast it is. I am scared."

"Well Ruth we are in good hands. . . God and the Fur Company so remember fear does not enter in here alright."

"Yes I know! But Emma the vastness of this area, it is unbelievable."

"Pay attention, looks like we have arrived."

Entering into Cantonment Leavenworth the travelers were greeted by a large group of men all talking at once asking them where they were from, where they are going, welcoming the ladies until MacGhie yells out, "People! Give these ladies some space! They are tired and some are injured. We need to get them settled in first."

"That is very true . . . men back off! Hey MacGhie you got one heck of a large group traveling with you."

"Norton Bruster, you ol' son of a gun, still hangin' around here!"

"Yea you got that right!" Norton said with a big smile.

"Good to see you and yes I sure do have a large group this time around."

"We will talk later MacGhie."

"Looking forward to it Norton."

Norton waves then begins to direct where everyone will go.

The ladies are shown into comfortable quarters of the barracks or "The Rookery" as it is called. The beds are a welcome site and Greta was first to lay down commenting on how wonderful it felt then in minutes, she was asleep. The other girls did the same after they unpacked a few things. Soon it was dinnertime and the ladies were summoned to dine. Upon entering the room, the men stand. Norton Bruster extending his arm toward an empty chair and says, "Mrs. Cooper, please sit here next to me."

"Oh thank you." She then looks at Doc Allen who looks a bit upset, she continues, "But I do believe Doc Allen has saved me a seat over there." Mr. Bruster smiles and leaves the table to attach his large arm to Greta's arm saying, "Mrs. Yancey let me assist you. This chair is closer for you."

Greta smiles saying "Thank you." She glances at Matt who looked displeased as she sits down and coffee is being poured for her.

"Norton is my name, Ma'am." He smiles showing his large straight teeth that seem to sparkle against his tan skin and white hair tightly pulled back.

As the girls enter the room the men of the fur company jump up to take the arms of the ladies whom they have been escorting for weeks and now have the opportunity to occupy their time. The men at the fort take their seats disappointed that they could not have these fine ladies at their table.

Norton says, "Josiah, you heading to the Otoe Village and then to the Pawnee Village?"

"That is the way I figured."

"Will you need Military escort to the Platte?"

I do not think so. We have a good size group here that can well handle themselves."

"Yes you do. How many men are traveling in your Company?"

"Close to fifty. Right Leavitt?

"Yes Sir at last count all were present and accounted for."

"I know this for sure Josiah; the American Fur Company that went days ahead of the Missionaries will be building bridges and preparing roads for the Missionary group. That will be of great help to you and your group."

"That is good news!"

"Then on to Fort William." Norton said.

"Yes. But why the look of concern?"

"Josiah, you know the Pawnee are deadly enemies to all Indians don't you?"

"Um . . . yes Bruster . . . but not in front of the ladies. We can discuss this at a later time."

"Oh sure of course. Not use to having fine ladies around this place." He looks at the ladies and was glad they did not hear any part of this conversation.

"Have any of you been west of the Missouri?" Colonel Longhorn questioned.

The ladies and Isaac said no. Greta said yes but years ago.

Norton says, "Welp, first time or hundredth time . . . it is a never ending site to behold. You are now in the great prairie. It does not end until you get to the Pacific and it extends north and south for thousands of miles. You will see."

As others talked amongst themselves Doc whispers, "I do love you Ellie Cooper." She whispers back, "And I love you William Allen." Both smile and continue eating.

"So Miss Emma, you look very nice and well rested." Tom says smiling.

"Thank you Tom. Well rested? How did I look before?"

Tom whispers, "Emma I am just making nice conversation." Then louder he says, "Hey this sowbelly sure taste good."

Emma smiles and agrees as she kicks him under the table.

The room they were in was a very large room with only the necessities in it for eating.

Conversations were continuing around the table as the Fur Company men finally got to enjoy the company of these fine ladies. After the short introductions one to another the talk is kept low-keyed and simple, as no one wanted to overpower the conversation.

When dinner ended, everyone went outside for some evening music and talk. The other men in the Cantonment joined in also. Norton begins the talk saying, "So you ladies are heading to Fort William and you come from Pennsylvania . . . that is a might piece to travel. You know, a while back we had two women come through here from New York heading to Fort Walla Walla, they are Missionaries. What were their names?"

Colonel Longhorn answered, "Eliza Spalding and Narcissa Whitman."

"Yes that is them. The first white women to travel this far west. Are you meeting with any missionaries Ma'am?"

Ellie smiled and said, "No but it is exciting. I thought we might be the first ones."

Colonel Longhorn smiled as he commented. "Actually there was one lady who came west with her husband, his name was Manuel de Lisa, a Spanish fur trader who established a post at the mouth of the Bighorn and at Fort Lisa. He was a very successful man to who ever entered Indian Country in the early days. He was a great asset to the government. That was around 1807 but his wife,

Mary, who they say spent the winter with him, that was winter of 1819-1820. However, Ma'am you are first to travel without men that are kin to you, except for your Son-in-law."

"Yes well we are fortunate to be traveling with Mr. MacGhie and the Fur Company." Greta politely smiled.

"You have some injured ladies. How did they get hurt?" Colonel commented.

Ellie looks at the girls then begins, "Yes, well, a few weeks back we had an episode with the Prairie Banditos and. . ."

The men of the Cantonment and their encounters with this notorious group interrupted her talking with what they knew of this group. Ellie and the girls were beside themselves listening to all the talk and not knowing which one to listen to first.

"Alright men let Mrs. Cooper talk." Shouted Colonel Longhorn.

They all apologize and then are quiet. Ellie begins again while coffee is offered around but her talking was short lived. Dr. Reynolds approached the group. Hearing what she was saying he politely says, "Ma'am, may I interrupt you for a moment?"

"Yes of course. What is it you need?"

"I would like to say something to these men."

"Yes go right ahead." Ellie said smiling.

"Men, you have been in many battles and you know when someone can handle themselves in a fight. Well I am here to tell you, as an eye witness, these nine ladies know well the art of battle."

"Um . . . Doctor Reynolds, that is not necessary . . ." Ellie again was interrupted as Doctor Reynolds continues . . . "Yes Ma'am it is very necessary. Now men, when I saw their Mother in hand to hand combat with an Indian, almost getting her hair removed and killed, these young ladies, sitting with us today, right here, had courage like I never saw. The determination that showed in their face to win this battle was intense. Picture this men . . . and I know each of you can . . . angry men riding horses at high speed yelling and hollering, creating a huge amount of dust and in the center of it all these ladies under cover,continually wiping dust from their burning eyes as they maintain the rhythm of load, aim, shoot, re-load, aim, shoot over and over again, hitting their target each time. While not knowing if their mother, lying on the ground was alive or dead. They stood their post. Even when injured they did what they could to win. Nine women fighting for their life and here they all sit as testament of that battle. Men, I tell you it was something marvelous to behold. When the fighting was over the Fur Company men stood up, called these ladies mountain material, and were proud to know them. Men, this is no yarn I am weaving. This is factual truth and any Fur Company man here can attest to it. You are sitting with some mighty important, highly respected ladies that have had some intense mountain man training. Who need no man to guide them. It's clear to me they have divine guidance! I am truly proud to know everyone of you. That is all I have to say. Thank you Ma'am."

Ellie was stunned and could only smile saying, "Well gentlemen, I certainly cannot top that. Thank you Doctor Reynolds."

More talk continues until Norton Bruster spoke loudly, "Men, we need to let these ladies get some rest. Clear out now. We will see you in the morning. Rest well."

"Thank you. Good night. You all have been very kind and we appreciate all you gentlemen have done for us. I know there is no way we could ever repay your kindness. We can only say thank you." Greta said and she stood up from the chair.

"Ma'am we do what we do because, well, because you ladies are a cut above the ordinary and we appreciate you.

Thank you Ma'am, we thank all of you for this wonderful opportunity to know you." Norton Bruster spoke smiling. "Now Ma'am may I have the honor of walking you to your room?"

Greta glances at Matt who was talking with someone else and paid no mind to what was going on so she answered, "That would be very nice of you Mr. Bruster. Thank you." smiling she attached her arm to his and he guided her to her room.

Matt did notice and was not happy but still made no never mind about the whole thing.

CHAPTER EIGHT

As the girls ready themselves for bed they talked about the evening and each one talked about the gentleman that sat next to them during dinner.

Greta finally says, "Girls get to bed. I will see you in the morning."

All say good night.

Come morning they were once again escorted to the table by the same men. The talk interrupted by MacGhie tapping his cup on the table to get the attention of everyone then said, "We are looking at 300 miles to the Otoe Village at the mouth of the Platte. We leave early tomorrow. Make sure you have all you need. Timber is found only along the river and great caution in making a fire. Once the prairie is a blaze, there is no stopping it. With the tall grass, it moves along like a wave of fire destroying everything in its path. And I do mean everything. We will leave at four in the morning. Any questions?"

And so the ordeal once again begins. Prepare for the leaving.

Emma and Claire rearrange the wagon when Katie and Ruth said they could ride their horses.

It was not long that the men showed up with extra blankets for the horses. Each girl was outfitted quite well as was Ellie and Greta. Seems the men know what is ahead of these fine women and want to make their travel as comfortable as possible. The ladies thanked the men of the Cantonment Leavenworth and bid them all farewell.

The group left promptly, on schedule, at four in the morning for the Otoe Village as the rain pounded on all the travelers again. They kept in mind of the riders who came in with news of better weather in the north. The travel was as before, to travel 12–15 miles per day and when they found a good spot they would lay over one day per week to rest the animals and wash clothes. Once the rain stopped and the weather was warmer, they were all very cautious of the fires they built making sure to put them out properly leaving no hot coals. The girls remembered what Mr. MacGhie said about the fires on the prairie. One particular evening the ladies sat around with the men and listened to them talk about the Prairie.

"This here tall grass can reach 8 or 9 feet. I remember on year, hey Leavitt you were with me, remember when this tall grass was up to our shoulders and we would loose site of everything when we went down in a small valley only to come up on the next bluff not knowing if Indians were coming up the other side. Then you would stand on that bluff and try to get your sites right whilst this here tall grass just a swayed with the wind."

"Yes I sure do remember that time. We were lucky to get out of that tall grass alive." Leavitt commented as he drank his coffee.

"We got to one area where the buffalo herd went through and that left us a wide and long path of trampled tall grass to travel on. That was a relief." Smitty said.

"I remember when all I saw was the hat of the fellow in front of me. I sure prayed not to see a feather." MacGhie commented.

The talk continued and the girls got a full idea of how dangerous it was in the beautiful tall grass of the prairie.

Good traveling was made and after about 18 days, they were at the Otoe Village.

"The Otoe's will help. You ladies just get into the canoe and they will take you across. We will bring everything else over." The girls helped Greta into a canoe made of skins and went across. The Missionaries welcomed them warmly.

"Hello, and welcome. Please come this way. You need to relax." A very joyful woman was speaking as she noticed Greta was injured. She carefully grabs Greta's arm to help as Ellie grabs Greta's other arm and the woman leads them to the Baptist Mission House saying, "I have tea on and some wonderful cakes we baked earlier, also biscuits. You know we Baptists love to eat. Oh excuse me, I am Abigail. You can introduce yourselves to the women in the House. There are more women but they have gone to the village with Reverend Merrill and his wife Eliza and will not be back for a few days."

"Thank you very much." says Ellie and Greta as the girls follow behind.

"We have humble dwellings here. Nothing like back east. However, you will be comfortable. Are you staying long?"

"I do believe we will continue on since it is so early in the day." Greta comments.

Abigail motions for one of the woman to get a pillow to put behind Greta as she sits down. Abigail continues, "Well then let us have a prayer or two for your continued safety and health."

Abigail waited for the tea to be poured and the pieces of cake, biscuits, and jam passed around. The Missionary women prayed in unison as the travelers listened. The girls thanked the women then small talk began. The missionaries were very interested in the travelers and asked many questions. Greta found it most tiring at this point in time but welcomed the joy of other women to talk too so she was gracious to answer any question especially the question about their lack of husbands.

The Missionaries informed the ladies of two more difficult streams they will have to cross before passing the Pawnee Villages. Since traveling with a large group of men the Yancey group was encouraged to hear the Pawnee would be of no threat. Still emphasizing caution as they are enemies to other Indians.

MacGhie, after seeing how the ladies were enjoying each other in long conversation, decided to stay the night getting a fresh start in the morning.

CHAPTER NINE

The large white home on the lands of Whispering Oaks once was a place of quiet and solitude. Now it was more like a Fort to be protected against hostiles. However, not hostile Indians, but one man Mr. Hadley.

The care of Emily was long and tedious. Lilly was good at caring for those in need and her brothers along with the other men were good at defending a friend in need. Lilly's sister Violet also came to tend Emily. Minton was happy that two women took charge over Miss Emily as she could then concentrate on the running of the house and feeding all these men.

"Mista Alistair, Sir, duz you tink Miss Lilly's brothers found Masta Matthew? Day ben gon long time."

"I am sure they will find him. I pray soon. This constant arguing with Hadley is wearing my patience thin."

"Yas Sir. It do dat to all us. He a bad man."

"That he is."

"Oh here I iz just a jawin' away holdin' youz cup of coffee. Here you goze Sir and some cake too."

"Thank you Minton. You have been most hospitable to all of us."

"Thank you Sar. Iz best git back to ma work"

Alistair nods his head and continues eating the cake. Mr. Howard rides up as he dismounts he is talking.

"Hello Alistair. Have you heard Hadley is on his way here to do more shouting?"

"He wears my patience thin."

"Yes as with all of us. May I ask Minton for a cup of coffee?"

Minton laughs as she comes out of the house saying, "Yes Sar, I don see you comin' an' node youz want coffee an' a piece of my strawberry cake. Iz was a step a head of youz."

"You certainly were Minton. Thank you very much."

Minton smiles as she hands him the coffee and cake then goes back into the house where there is much work going on. Minton had all the drapes pulled back and tied so the men could look out better. She had Able bring in more chairs to set about. As she buzzed around the house she heard talking but paid no mind to what was being said.

"With Hadley coming here so much he has left the other plantations alone."

"I would think so. I have not heard any one having trouble Alistair. He must be concentrating on this one only."

"Yes until he gets what he wants then he will be after someone else."

"I would suspect he will go after you next Alistair."

"You are right about that. I would deal with him very differently though."

"I think we all would. Have you heard anything form Edward and Clint?"

"No nothing. I am not too concerned. Once they are sure of the direction it will not take those men long to find Matthew." "And knowing Matthew once he hears this trouble the distance will be shortened considerably." The men agree and wait for another foolish encounter with Hadley.

CHAPTER TEN

Ellie and Greta talk as they go along the trail, "Greta, this is not as bad as I thought. The rolling hills are not steep so the wagons travel over them fairly well. Look at all that land and sky. Never ending land and never ending sky. I never thought the eye could see so far, like hundreds of miles in one look. How are you doing back there?"

"I am doing. You know if I had just the slightest inkling of what had happened to us I may not have traveled this far. Actually, Doc did try to warn me and I just did not listen."

"You can not fault yourself for anything that happened. And you cannot carry any regrets with you either. Besides it is not your nature to carry on so." Ellie said as she would look out over the terrain and then back at Greta.

"Oh I know it Ellie, and it is wonderful for the girls to see this grand land. But my God Ellie, what kind of fate lies ahead for us. What—", Greta was interrupted by Ellie.

"Greta! Do you hear yourself? Stop it right now. This is not like you. Not like you at all! Are you God? We are following His plan, correct. Then stop trying to second guess Him and just go back to trusting God as he leads the way."

"You are absolutely right Ellie! What was I thinking? My thinking must have gone topsy-turvy with my head hurting all the time. I can be just as silly as my girls."

"You sure can be and what is this about your head hurting?" Ellie said.

"Oh ever since that attack it has been hurting but I just figured it was part of the injury that needs time to heal." Greta said adjusting herself a little to look out the back of the wagon. She sees the bluffs and the tall grass and blue sky with whimsical cloud formations and the vast land that runs into the sky.

"Have you told Doc?"

Greta turns to Ellie and says, "Oh sure I did. But it all takes time to heal."

"Well at least he knows about it. Mr. MacGhie is coming. Hello Mr. MacGhie!" Ellie says as she waves to him.

"Hello Ma'am, I would like you to follow me in a few minutes and I will show you how to line up your wagons."

He rides over to his men and a few of them ride ahead about a quarter of a mile and make a circle away from the river. MacGhie then rides back to Ellie, "Ma'am, you just follow me. We will circle around those men and line up each wagon next to them. I will tell you when to stop."

"Alright." Ellie thinks, 'now what is so special about this circle?' She follows and lines up according to what he said. Confused Ellie says, "Mr. MacGhie . . . you left a large opening between these two wagons and why so far from the river?"

"Well first we are far from the river incase it rises in the storm and the opening will be where we will stack all the packs from the mules."

Ellie looks at how they are situated and before she could finish climbing down off the wagon MacGhie was back saying, "Ma'am do not set up your tents just yet. I will get back to you about that . . . just go ahead with your evening fire and hobbling the animals."

"Very well. I will hold all questions."

"Thank you Ma'am." He rides off to the men's camp area.

Ellie gives the usual instruction and does not think any more about what was said.

"MacGhie . . . I saw you set the wagons. You are expecting a bad storm aren't you?" Cooper said as he set the pot for coffee and hung the stew pot while Brave Eagle built a fire.

"Yes, I have been watching that storm line hoping it would move south. I do not think it will. Should be upon us in two days at the most. We will not make it to The Pawnee Village in time. We could have been sheltered well in their lodges. Now we will have to make the best of it."

"Do you really think the Pawnee would have sheltered us? This will be rough on the ladies."

"Come to think of it, it is probably better that we are not near them. Considering their dislike of other Indians, not to mention the white folks. I know this will be hard on the ladies, Cooper. We will need to help them secure everything down. We can use the wagons for breaking some of the wind. Winslow come here."

"Yes Sir."

"We will need extra rope to secure those wagons and peg them into the ground. Take some men and start now. Cooper will you speak to your mother and fill her in?"

"I will do that now." Tom Cooper heads over to his mothers camp.

"So that is the plan Ma. You girls listen to how they say to secure your tents."

"Securing is securing right?" Katie spoke.

"Katie . . . these winds can be pretty bad. They are coming right at you in a straight line and nothing in its path to block any of it. You do not have that in the mountains. Mountains break up some of the winds so do the trees. Out here in the open it is different."

"Oh, I am sorry. I guess I understand more now and that is why we are lower than the bluffs?"

Emma spoke up, "Tom is it that serious?"

"Could be." Tom said as Doc walked up. "And yes Katie. The wind will go over the bluffs somewhat. Of course these bluffs are not as big as we would like them to be at a time like this."

The girls look at the approaching storm in the distance. Ellie picked up a pan and said, "I will make more flapjacks and we can eat them during the storm."

"Put that wood stove in your tent." Doc said.

"That is a lot of trouble for just one day Doc." Ellie said.

Tom put his hand on his Mothers shoulder and said, "Mother, these storms can last a week . . . you best have dry wood and girls, when you get a chance pick up a lot of dried buffalo chips for the fire. Pull in some provisions for all of you. Put the tarps on the ground and part way up the side of the tents to keep the wetness out."

Some of the girls argue the point about the stove and a weeklong storm but Ellie quieted them down as she said, "Girls, these men know the prairie storms we do not. Do as they say with no grumbling."

"Yes we know but we thought the storms were done with." Katie said with arms folded.

"Now you are being silly. Can we predict what the weather is going to do or when? Just do as you are told alright." Ellie said as she went to the fire.

The stove was set up in the larger tent. Ellie transferred hot coals from the outside fire to the stove and kept it going. Quilts and blankets were brought in along with changes of clothing. A place was set up for Greta. She was not moved there yet as she wanted to enjoy the nice weather while it lasted. The girls fixed up an area where she could watch everyone working. Her head hurt more than the other wounds but she did not complain . . . she surmised she would just have to wait for the body to heal up. When camp was set up the girls went in all directions looking for buffalo chips. Some carried buckets others baskets. Katie was walking with Marie when they stopped to pick up quite a few in one area. "Can you believe we are really picking up buffalo chips? This is disgusting if you ask me."

"Well gee Katie, to keep a fire going this is what we have to do. This stuff is not going to hurt you." Marie said as she was filling her bucket.

"I know it won't hurt me. I prefer wood."

"If you see wood pick it up. But I do not think you will find any out here. Maybe some wild Indians like them Pawnee the men were talking about."

Katie jumped up off the ground to look around saying, "That is not funny. We could be captured. Let's get back to camp, now!"

Marie saw Katie walking away and shouted, "I was only teasing you. Wait for me! Did you get a lot of buffalo chips? Ellie wanted a lot."

Katie said nothing and just hurried back to camp looking around and thinking, 'how could any one see any thing in this tall grass. They could be laying down waiting to jump us.' She hurried all the more almost running and looking all around and not waiting for Marie who finally caught up and they made it back to camp with Marie laughing.

Ellie saw the girls hurrying back and questioned what was going on. Katie told her what Marie had said and Marie got a bit scolded for that. But Marie could not stop laughing at Katie.

While Cooper and Doc relax by the fire waiting for the pot of coffee to get done MacGhie walks up and says, "Some of the men were talking about you Tom, they say you know the mountains as good as the best of them . . . like Bridger and those other mountain men."

"Yep, I have gone with the best and gone it alone too. Would rather travel with others, much safer."

"Is it true you are going with these ladies to where they are going? And I heard it is deep in Indian country."

"Yep." Cooper leans forward to check the coffee, happy to find it done he pours for Doc making a motion toward MacGhie.

"Yes, I will have a cup. Thanks. Then those ladies are heading for a pack of trouble and you along with 'em. Indian trouble."

"I know but you have seen their determination." Cooper pours himself a cup. Doc nods his head in agreement about their determination.

"And where in those mountains are they going to make their home? I cannot figure that one out, even though Mrs. Yancey showed me a map. Still cannot figure the area."

"They are heading for Seth Yancey's cabin."

"Yancey's cabin? Man that is right in Indian country. Do they know that?"

"Don't suppose they do."

"Then Cooper . . . you go over there and tell them they cannot go. You tell them now!"

Doc looks at MacGhie and says, "Now MacGhie . . . you tell me just how much good that will do. They will not listen to anyone. Back in Earleysburg, many folk talked to them but they left anyways and there is the living proof right over there. Right there tending their own camp. I tell you MacGhie . . . they will go into Indian country and insist on making a new home. No doubt about that at all, they do not listen to anyone when it comes to their quest."

"You two are that serious?" MacGhie said looking very surprised.

"Yes we are."

"Oh wow! This is not good at all! Listen, to my understanding Seth Yancey had the acceptance from the Indians to build a cabin in their area. Mrs. Yancey is not Seth Yancey and neither are his girls. And they are all unmarried!"

"Yes MacGhie we know that. Oh, one is married. Want some muffins? Ruth brought them over awhile ago." Cooper hands a large pan filled with sweet muffins to

MacGhie. He takes one then Cooper set the pan down in front of himself.

"What I am getting at Cooper and Doc . . . is their bravery alone will stir up the young bucks and the Chief will send them to propose marriage." MacGhie sits on the other side of Cooper to be closer to the muffins as he realizes the goodness of them.

Doc looks at MacGhie and he sits down next to Cooper on the other side and closer to the muffins saying, "You really think that will happen?"

Cooper says, "Bound to happen. It is the Indian way . . . yep . . . bound to happen."

The three men watch the girls while they eat their muffin in hand. Having the same thought . . . what will these girls do when that time comes and these men know it will come about.

Emma finished anchoring the last tent strap, stands up saying, "That will do. Looks like we are done. . . Katie go over to Ellie and see if she needs help."

"Katie do this, Katie do that! Just because I am feeling better. . . ."

"Never mind, I will go, you go write in your journal."

Emma goes by Ellie and asks if she needs help.

"Yes. You can fill this pot with water for me."

"Sure will. Say Ellie, why are those three sitting so peculiar?"

" Who? Where?" Ellie says as she looks around.

"There . . . Tom, Doc, and Mr. MacGhie sitting by that camp fire." Emma just nods her head in that direction. Ellie looks over at the three men then shrugs her shoulders saying, "I do not know. Could be they just stopped talking and looked up at the same time. Know what I mean."

"Yes. Still they look peculiar." Emma said as she goes to get the water.

Doc stands up, "Nope it will not work!"

Matt walks up and pours himself a cup of coffee, grabs a muffin while saying, "What will not work Doc?"

"The Indians proposing to the Yancey girls."

"What!"

Cooper fills in Matt who looks at the girl. Just before Cooper finishes all four men are now looking at the girls.

"Look at that Ellie, Mr. Braummer must have a crick in his back . . . he is bent and not moving."

"Yes and once again they are looking here."

"I do not know what they are . . . oh look . . . Mr. Braummer is finally sitting down. He must have been pouring coffee for all of them."

"Well let us finish up this stew. Thanks for the water." Emma pours some of the water in to the pot as Ellie stirs it.

Matt says, "You are just making a joke right?"

"No Matt. We are serious." Doc said.

"Dadburnit! We do not need that kind of trouble . . . those girls will have to cut their hair and dress like men. That is the only thing they can do." Matt says as he slaps his knee.

Doc looks at Matt saying, "Alright Matt . . . now that will not work and you know it. They have to bathe some time and that will sure tell them Indians they are not men."

"Oh yeh . . . well . . . what are we going to do? Cooper, what can we do? MacGhie?"

"Hey Matt, do not look at me . . . I have no idea right now." Doc said.

Cooper responds, "Same here."

"Neither do I." MacGhie says sitting down again. They continue enjoying the muffins and thinking what to do. They see Brave Eagle and call him over.

Cooper begins, "Brave Eagle . . . those wonderful girls will be making their home at the Seth Yancey's cabin."

The Indian looks at Cooper surprised as Cooper continues, "Yes . . . it is true and do you know what will take place when they make that cabin their home . . . the trouble will be heard all over the mountain range. And you know the proposals of marriage will be never ending."

Matt looks at Cooper saying, "Never ending?"

Cooper slaps his knee saying, "Yup . . . never ending!"

The girls help get Greta comfortable sitting near them and prepare her plate of food.

"Look there Emma, now the Indian. What the heck is the matter with those men?" Ellie looks at all the other men and they were all sitting in their areas or doing odd jobs. It was only MacGhie, Cooper, Mr. Braummer, Doc, and Brave Eagle who were looking in their direction. "Oh just ignore them . . . Emma hand me your plate . . . girls get your plates ready so we can sit and relax with this fine meal."

"Stop laughing Brave Eagle . . . this is serious. I do not see the humor in it at all." Matt said, "All the mountains ranges will hear of this. . . "

"Yes Sir. That is what I said."

Brave Eagle continues to laugh. As each one of these men think of the girls . . . bullheaded, determined, beautiful girls each one begins to laugh and soon they are all laughing.

The girls look over at the laughing men and Ruth says, "The joke must have just sunk in."

The other girls agree and they continue enjoying the stew as the five men attempt to drink their coffee and eat the muffins in the mist of laughter.

As time went on and the men stopped laughing and began the small talk again, Tom went to check the animals and motioned for Brave Eagle to come along. When far enough away from camp Tom said, "Well my friends . . . are you thinking what I am thinking . . . this storm is going to be a bad one."

"Bad yes. Move in fast and strong. Animals run."

"We hobbled them good so they will not get far."

"Watch girls close."

"Will do . . . hey that is why our tent is next to theirs."

"Yes. Can hear screams better. Know when in trouble."

Tom chuckles saying, "Oh alright . . . but I do not think they are going to scream. It is still good to be close by."

Brave Eagle smiles and continues checking the animals.

Evening was upon them and Katie was restless, "Emma. May I please walk around outside? This waiting is very uncomfortable."

"Yes Katie, go outside. You are fidgeting around too much."

Katie goes out into the dark. The only light is from the campfires. She walks around a little looking at the coming storm and thinks, 'why are we even out here? I do not like it. I am scared and I cannot even talk to my mother."

Matt was sitting by the fire watching Katie walk around knowing she was scared. However, his thought went to his sister, Emily and if she received his letter about heading west to find Greta. His thoughts were also of Greta and their earlier discussion, then the thoughts drift back to his sister and the plantation his grandparents called "Whispering Oaks." His thoughts were broken when Katie said, "Mr. Braummer. May I sit by you? This storm kind of bothers me."

"Yes, sure you can."

She sits right close and he puts his arm around her saying. "Kind of hard not being able to talk to your mother isn't it?"

"Yes Sir. Mr. Braummer will my mother be the same as before or will she stay different?"

Matt looks at her and for the first time he saw what Greta has been saying about the girls needing her. He remembered when he sat with his sister when she was scared and he was glad Katie came to him.

"Mr. Braummer, will my mother be like this. . . "

"I am sorry Katie, but I cannot possibly answer that question. I do not think Doc could honestly answer it either. We just have to wait for her to heal. At a time like this I think your Ma would be reading her Bible for comfort, peace, and answers."

"Oh Mr. Braummer, that may work for her or Emma but not me. I cannot. . . "

"Katie . . . I understand what you mean. I really do. However, after long thoughts about your Ma and the Bible, and I have known your Ma a long time. I have concluded that to have the Faith and understanding she has, you just stick with it . . . reading it a lot and understanding gets stronger."

Katie looked a bit disgusted, "Really? You honestly believe there is something to reading it. Getting answers?"

"I do not read it much . . . I will be honest with you on that. But, I don't know . . . it is like your Ma has a royal flush and we hold a pair."

Katie looked confused saying, "What?"

"Umm, maybe this will help. She has got the whole receipt and the ingredients . . . we have half the receipt and no ingredients."

"Oh! I see what you mean now. Then the Bible is like a receipt and ingredients together. The more you read the more ingredients you get to use."

Matt looks surprised at her and says, "Yes exactly."

"Thank you Mr. Braummer."

"Sure glad to be of some help." Matt relaxes and sips his coffee.

"May I sit here longer with you and watch the lightening in the distance?"

"You sure can."

Katie snuggles closer and Matt feels what he has not felt in a long time . . . a love like he has with his sister. He gives Katie a squeeze saying, "Thank you Katie."

"For what?"

He smiled at her saying, "For bringing back memories I long forgot."

They both smile and watch the distant lightening and low rumble of thunder every so often. Matt's thoughts are of his sister, Katie feels secure, and safe . . . feelings she had lost have now returned.

CHAPTER ELEVEN

Rolling dark clouds came closer and closer as the wind picked up its speed. The cattle lay in calm nature with a "mooing" sound ever so often. The tall grass moves like waves of the sea as the wind travels over and down the bluffs.

"Emma." Marie said as she watched the cows. "Do you find it peculiar to see the cows relaxing like that?"

"No, not really. It is what they do before a storm because during the storm the lightening and thunder scare them and they run here and there." Emma commented as she sat on the blanket watching the clouds roll in.

"We are relaxing before this storm comes too."

"Yes Marie, but when the storm does comes I do not think we will be running around in all directions. We will be on guard in case anything should happen. And please do not ask what could happen because I do not know."

"I will not ask. That sky looks mean." Marie says as she studies the clouds and color of the sky.

"Yes it does. Soon we will be going into the tent. Are you alright Marie?" Emma said as she reaches for Maries hand to hold.

"Yes. I know we will be alright . . . we have to be . . . right?"

"Hey you two girls! How are you doing?"

"Oh hello Tom. We are just watching the sky."

"Yes Mr. Tom and that storm is coming closer and closer. Did you hear the thunder?" Marie perks up and looks intently at the approaching clouds listening for the thunder.

"I hear. That is why I came over. Emma get your sisters together and into the tent. No need to be out here scrambling in the rain."

Marie jumps up, grabs her blanket, and says, "You do not have to tell me twice. That thunder is a lot closer. See you in the tent Emma." And off Marie ran.

"Alright." Emma stands up brushing her skirt off saying, "I will go tell the others."

"Good. If you need anything Emma, just call out." He pauses a bit and clumsily continues, "I am in the tent next to yours . . . Brave Eagle . . . and I are in there."

"Thank you Tom. That is good to know." Emma says as she smiles.

Tom picks up the blanket, shakes it and hands it to Emma. Their hands brush up against each other and they quickly part company to do what each must do. Emma thinks 'So what if our hands touched. That does not mean anything. Why am I flushed, oh, this is ridicules.' She sees Ruth and says, "Ruth go tell Alex and Isaac we need to get into the tents. I will get Claire and Anne."

"I saw Marie and Katie go in the tent already. Ma and Ellie are in also. Are you alright? You look a little flushed."

"Yes of course I am alright. And I am not flushed!"

"Emma you are-"

"Enough with the flush!" Emma says and quickly heads out to find Claire and Anne who were sitting with Doc and Matt listening to the other men talk of their travels west.

"Girls . . . time to get in the tent."

"Yes alright." Claire said, "This has been interesting. Marie would have enjoyed listening to the conversation. You alright Emma? You look flushed."

Emma slumps her shoulders then sternly says, "Well you two can tell her all about it once in the tent. And I am not flushed! Now let's go."

Doc said as he was getting up to look at her, "Emma you do look a bit flushed-"

"Doc please, we have to get to our tents."

The girls are already heading back and Emma rushes but not enough to catch up with them. She thinks, 'Flushed! Indeed! I just brushed his hand so what.'

Raindrops could be felt now and the men go to their tents. Once inside the rain did not take long to beat hard and loud against the tent walls. The thunder was loud and shook the ground. It was now dark in the afternoon and the tent continued to shake against the wind but stood its course. Alex and Isaac were in their own tent warm and cozy knowing that in time they will have to go to the larger tent to eat. However, in the mean time, they enjoyed this time together along with the coffee Isaac got from Ellie and some flapjacks and preserves. Alex said, "Do you miss your family Isaac?"

"Yes I do. I hope I will see them again."

"Oh Isaac I hope so too. You have a wonderful family." At that they just cuddled up together and enjoyed the little meal.

The storm raged on for hours and a new noise was heard.

"What is that sound? Claire said as she intently listened. The tent was dimly lit as no one was reading. They were just talking and listening to the storm.

"What sound? All I can hear is rain and wind on the tent walls." Anne said.

"No listen will you."

"Stop it Claire!" Emma said.

"Really! Listen! I am not fooling around." Claire is leaning and intensely listening.

The girls being disgusted and not wanting to bother decided to humor Claire and make like they were intently listening by cupping their hands over there ears and leaning forward as if to really be listening.

"I hear something." Greta says which now changed the girls' attitude and they did listen more intently.

Claire crawls over to the tent door saying, "It sound like it is right outside."

Emma laughs a little saying, "Oh it is probably that Mr. Tom Cooper trying to scare us in this awful storm."

Claire gets closer, "You think so, Emma? You really think he would come out in a storm like this just to scare us?"

"I am sure of it." Emma says looking at the other girls who giggle a little but just sit and listen.

"Well if it is him he will be very surprised when I open this flap up." Claire said as she slowly unties the flaps and grabs hold of them. The girls get ready to jump on who ever is out there. Anne goes to the other side of the door and grabs a flap to help Claire get them open wide and fast. They both pull them open the rain and wind blow in as they are ready to grab the person, when they scream, something dark runs in . . . all the girls scream. Ellie and Greta are yelling to close the flaps while the wind continues to drive the rain inside the tent. Then the lanterns go out.

Marie and Katie start screaming, "It is a bear! It is a bear!"

Alex and Isaac hear the screaming and Isaac hurries to get his boots and coat on before going out into the storm. In another tent Tom Cooper and Brave Eagle hear the screaming. Cooper looks at his smiling friend who says, "See girls scream."

"Yea well let's go over there and see what it is all about."

Isaac, Cooper, and Brave Eagle arrive and grab the flaps attempting to enter into the tent but cannot. The girls are running around and something black is chasing them. Cooper holds the lantern high, grabs Emma's arm and says, "Slow down and hold this up." He leaps in and grabs the black object. He hears the screams of "It's a bear! It's a bear!" realizing this bear is very thin . . . he grabs it around the head and neck area as one of the girls scream out, "The bear is eating him!" The girls were screaming as they ran outside in the storm knocking over Isaac as other men come running. Matt and Doc help Isaac up and try to make sense of what the girls are saying. Other men try to get to the tent but the girls are running in all directions and in circles bumping into each other in front of the blowing flaps. Emma is still holding the lantern high but is now outside of the tent frozen in place, the lantern is out. The girls are thinking the worse then realize Ellie and Greta are still inside witnessing this awful feeding of a man. There is no settling the girls down so the men start grabbing them and move them to the rear of the crowd. Matt, Doc, and Isaac are also grabbing them and moving them. Lightening was their only source of light to focus on what is happening in the tent as the flaps blew open in the wind. The men are now prepared to rush the tent when they see lanterns being lit and Cooper squatting down next to something black. Brave Eagle says, "It is dog." They all stand stunned with the roaring wind and rain beating against them as they try to hear what Brave Eagle is saying. He repeats louder, "It dog." Shocked, Doc says, "He's gone?" Others move in closer trying to hear while shielding their faces from the wind and rain.

Matt and Mr. MacGhie say together, "Who is gone?"

Isaac puts his head down just moving it back and forth in sadness thinking 'poor Mr. Cooper.'

The girls console each other thinking what was it that ate Mr. Cooper. Emma still standing with the lantern high thinks, 'My friend is gone?'

Cooper stands up and yells at everyone, "It is a dog . . . a dog . . . see." He grabs a lantern and shines it above the two-year-old black dog eating pieces of bread.

Many of the men repeat "A dog?"

The girls look at each other in shock saying "A dog?" Then excited, they run into the tent shouting, "A dog! It is a dog?"

Ellie begins to build the fire hotter, and then she thanks the men and chases them off saying, "I am sorry for this entire ruckus. Go now, get yourselves dry, and relax. We will be all right now. Thank you for your help." She then ties up the tent flaps and look at the girls saying, "Now get out of those wet clothes, and leave the dog alone. I will get the tea going. We need to hang these clothes and blankets up. Greta are you alright?"

"Sure. I did not get wet at all thanks to all the bedding thrown on me and I did not get to see Tom's face eaten up. By the way Tom how are you feeling?"

"Oh my goodness, I forgot you and Brave Eagle and Isaac were still in here. Good thing the girls do not listen to me all the time." Ellie smiles.

"So are we Ma. We better get out of here and dry off ourselves. Are you girls calmed down now?"

"Yes Tom. I think we are. Thank you and thank you also Brave Eagle and Isaac for your help." Emma says as she unties the tent flaps to let them leave giving Tom a nice smile.

"No problem. Should you need anything else just scream." They laugh and leave the tent.

Ellie says, "Oh, Isaac, do you and Alex have enough coffee or would you like some tea?"

"Tea would be better right now."

Ellie says, "When the tea is done I will bring it over."

"Or you can just call out and I will come for it. Now I best get to Alex and fill her in on the excitement."

He leaves and Emma ties up the flaps as she thinks how brave Tom was to jump on that animal not knowing what it was and then hearing that is was a bear, he continued. Could it be true what that Frenchman said about the Mountain Man? Her sisters attempting to name the dog disrupt her thoughts. They could not agree on one name.

Greta speaks up, "I think we should name him Sergeant. He was top in this battle and came out unwounded."

"That is a perfect name Mama." Marie says as Anne, Katie, Ruth, Claire, and Emma agree.

So Sergeant is now part of the family and he feels very welcome and finds a comfortable spot by the stove. He lies down and watches his new family. When the tea was done, Ellie went to the tent of Isaac and Alex and visited awhile with them.

Tom and Brave Eagle were sitting in their tent with dry clothes on and Brave Eagle said, "Nice smile Emma have."

Tom looks at him saying, "Yes it is, so what."

"Early today you look red in face."

"Awe it was the sun."

"Tom, no sun just clouds." Brave Eagle smiles.

"I am turning in, good night."

"Me call you Cooper Red Face. Want one feather?"

"Funny real funny. Good night my friend."

It rained for four days. On the sixth day, they were ready to travel again.

CHAPTER TWELVE

The group continue to travel west through the tall grass of the prairie. Luckily it was not as tall as the men spoke of before.

"Emma just look at this land. For miles and miles just grass and sky. Sort of frightening don't you think?"

"Yes Ruth. But what is more frightening is what lies ahead. When I think of what our life was like back home and then try to think of what our life will be in the west. I just cannot imagine . . . there is no way of knowing."

"I know what you mean. Hey look at it this way . . . we are at the right time of the year . . . the grass is great for our animals and we do not need to use the feed which will be used in the winter. I think we are in good standings and it can only get better." Ruth said as she pointed to Ellie approaching.

"I do have to agree with you on that. Everyone is healed from their wounds, and we have been provided great protection. Hello Ellie. What do you think of this land?" Emma said.

"Big and wide. I was on my way to see your mother but I must talk to Mr. MacGhie first."

The girls continue looking around and talking as Ellie has her talk with MacGhie then she is on to Greta's wagon. The three big Conestoga wagons moved along the rough ground with ease. Isaac's smaller wagon moved along just fine also. Although for some one riding inside it was not steady at all.

"Hello Greta. I just spoke to Mr. MacGhie; he says the Pawnee Village is just a few days ahead of us. Hey Greta, I am talking to you."

"I am sorry were you speaking to me?" Greta then went back to folding up a quilt.

"Yes I was. I said we have a few days till we get to the Pawnee Village."

"Oh that is nice. Is that where we are going?"

Ellie looked puzzled. "Yes, that is where we are going. Are you alright?"

Greta stops folding the quilt and says, "Excuse me . . . but do I know you?"

"What! Greta what are you talking about?"

Greta smiles politely saying, "Who is Greta? Clearly you can see there is no one in here but me. Why not try one of the other wagons."

"Oh my!" Ellie begins to wave her arms frantically at Doc yelling, "Doc, Doc! Get over here quick!"

Doc rides up, "What is all the excitement?"

"Just listen to Greta. Better yet, go talk to her, yes go ahead . . . talk to her."

"Sure. Hello Greta. Are you comfortable?"

Greta moves the quilt to another spot in the wagon and looking up says, "Hello. What is your name?"

"What is my name? Stop being silly. Now seriously how are you?" Doc said not in the mood for playing.

"I would like to tell you but I do not know since I do not know what happened to me. Can you tell me Sir? Why am I in this wagon?"

Looking confused Doc says, "You do not know what happened to you?"

"No Sir. Except my head does hurt. Can you tell me what I am doing in this wagon in the middle of nowhere?" Greta said as she looked around the area.

Doc looked at her then at Ellie who says shaking her head up and down, "See I told you . . . just talk to her. What is wrong with her Doc?"

"Alright, this is not funny, come on Greta . . . enough is enough. The jokes on me ha ha ha. Now how are you?"

"I beg your pardon Sir. . . "

Ellie interrupts, "Doc, she is not fooling. She does not know who she is! Let alone who we are!"

Doc looks at Greta as he gets off his horse and tells Ellie to have Ruth stop the wagons.

"Greta, Ma'am, may I feel your head?"

"If you must. However, if you are looking for that other person she is not here with me. I told that other lady I am in here alone."

"Yes I know that Ma'am."

Greta leans forward to the end of the wagon. Doc begins to move his hands over her head and stops, feeling a large lump just above her ear. Ellie comes back as Doc says, "A bump a very large bump. Do you know what happened, Ma'am?"

"I do remember the wagon hitting a large hole or something that threw me up against the back of the wagon where I hit my head."

"Will she be alright?"

"I do not know. Greta . . . look at me."

Greta looks at Doc while in a musical way pronounces her name out. "Grreetaaa . . . Ggrretaaaa." She moves her head in different positions as she singsongs her name, "Grrreeetaaaaaa . . . that is an odd name. You keep calling me that. Grrretaaaaaaa, hum, strange little name." She continues repeating the name as if she were tasting a new food and trying to decide if she likes it or not. Doc was attempting to analyze her when Matt walked up saying, "Hey how are things going?"

Doc froze in place then said, "Ellie go with Matt and get some water please."

"Why . . . I am not thirsty."

Doc puts his hands on Matts shoulders to stop him from coming closer and says, "You are not . . . oh well . . . Ellie is and she wants to talk to you."

"Then talk."

Greta looks at Matt in a very accepting manner saying, "Woo, now who is this handsome strap of a man?" Her interest is obvious as she says, "Come closer to me. I want to melt in your eyes. . . ." She moves seductively closer to the edge of the wagon.

Doc interrupts, "Um yes, yes . . . please sit back down so I can continue checking your head."

"Why Mr. Doc let him rub my head and. . . "

Just then, Doc puts his hand on her head and shoves her back down. He turns to Matt and Ellie saying, "Go get the water."

Matt stands firm and says, "Wait a minute here! You see Greta wants me to stay . . . Greta . . . you look different."

"Grrrreetaa." She then looks at Matt. "What is your name handsome? I like your muscles. . . "

"It is Matt. You know that! Say what kind of game is this?" He looks at Doc confused.

"Mmmaaaat . . . that is a different kind of name . . . like Grrreetaaa. Small names." She looks at Matt, "You sure are nice to look at Mmmaaaat."

Matt cannot take anymore and sternly he says, "Alright. Jokes over. You can stop acting so odd Greta."

"Grrrrrrreeetaaaaa." She sings as she relaxes back into the wagon.

"This is no joke Matt. Go with Ellie now."

Ellie grabs his arm pulling him away when Greta gets that strange look in her eyes saying, "Woo woo, you do not want to go away good looking. Stay here."

"Ellie get him out of here! Now!"

She pulls Matt away as Doc is having a hard time keeping Greta in the wagon. "I fancy him Mr. Doc, where is he going?"

"Just sit back down and relax. Please listen to me."

As Ellie and Matt walk away, "Matt, just listen to me before you say a word."

"Sure sure but this is. . . "

"Matt listen!" Ellie then fills him in on what is going on with the bump on her head.

"You mean she not only does not know who we are but she does not know who she is either?"

"Afraid so."

"Holy green earth! Things just keep getting better and better! How did this happen? Hey, she will know me right. I mean . . . when this passes she will know who I am . . . who we all are, right?"

"I do not know. Here have some water."

"I need something stronger than water. Does not know us at all. Not even the girls?"

"I would not think so. Yet she has not seen a one of them today so I could not say."

"That is why she is acting so. . . " He smiles as he thinks of Greta . . . how she was acting toward him, and then realizes Ellie is still with him, "Well, you know what I mean."

"Yes I do . . . quite out of character for her."

Matt smiles, "Yes very!"

As Emma and Ruth approach the wagon Greta see's a familiarity but does not know who they are.

"You girls look very familiar but I do not know where I would know you from. Have we met before?"

The girls look confused and could not speak for a moment which gave Doc the perfect opportunity to grab the girls by their arms and lead them away saying to Greta, "Well it will come to you in due time. Just relax and rest. And you girls help Ellie make some coffee, tea, or what ever and get your sisters to help too. Just keep away from your mother for awhile please."

Emma tries to stop, "Wait Doc! What did my mother mean?"

"Please Emma, just talk to Ellie . . . now keep going."

Doc gives Emma and Ruth a little shove and returns to Greta.

"Coffee will be done soon. Just sit back and relax."

"Sir . . . who are those girls? I am sure I know them and look," pointing to the other five girls, "Those girls over there, they look like I should know them but I do not . . . do I."

"In due time Greta. One-step at a time and your first step is to heal. The rest will be conquered."

"I suppose there is nothing I can do about anything except listen to you."

Doc was relieved to hear her say that and says, "Thank you! That I really appreciate. Now just lay back and relax."

"Mr. Doc, this dog has not left my side. What is his name?"

"Sergeant." Doc said petting him, "He is a very good dog."

"That is a nice name for him. Sergeant." She lays back just petting his head and then says, "Mr. Doc . . . may I ask you something? It may be nothing but a name keeps coming into my head. Do you know someone by the name of Seth?"

Doc was shocked to hear her say that name. He just patted her hand and said, "Yes I do but in due time. Now relax. I will see about the coffee."

Greta smiled and did as Doc asked.

Doc turns to see Emma in a rage and the other girls very confused. He thinks, 'oh great just what I need . . . seven crazed girls.'

The girls run up to Doc asking question after question all at the same time. He raised his arms saying, "Hold on just settle down please, and I will explain. This is hard enough for all of us now please sit back down. Matt help me out here will you?"

"Hey Doc come on . . . if I was female I would be right with them shouting questions at you. Therefore, I will not be any help to you at all. Just start explaining."

"Thank you very much. Ellie please?"

"Girls sit down and give Doc some breathing room. You too Matt. How is Doc supposed to say anything when your mouths are going wild? Sit down!" Ellie said sternly.

Emma goes to get coffee and Ellie stops her, "I said sit down. I will get you all coffee. Now quiet!"

"Thank you Ellie. Here goes, please do not say anything until I am done. Your Mother, Greta, has a bump on her head. When I asked where she got it from she remembered the wagon hitting a hole and she fell against the back of the wagon hitting her head. That is all she remembers after that. I have no idea how long this memory loss can last. I have no idea if she will recover completely or at all. I do know you girls need to keep your heads calm and please do not rush up to her, do not ask her questions and for heaven sakes do not ask her if she remembers you. She said you all looked familiar and that is very good. I have not told her who you are or where we are going or where we are coming from. I told her in due time she would know. Right now, I want her to relax and heal. Let her body deal with one thing at a time. Is that perfectly clear?"

Ruth gets up to go to her and Doc says, "No Ruth, leave her be . . . she needs to be alone right now."

Katie then stands up saying, "Well I do not need to be alone! I need my mother back. . . I need her to know who I am! See we should have never left! We should have never come out here! We were better off back home! Back home where Mother knew us all." Katie stares out over the vastness of the land and tears swell up in her eyes.

"Shut up Katie! Just shut your mouth right now or I will crack you one right in that mouth of yours!" Claire said as she sat staring at Katie and Katie, with clenched fists still staring off.

Matt speaks up, "Claire stop now. All of you just stop it. Your mother does not need to hear or see you all carry on like this. In addition, Katie . . . your mother made the decision to move west. I think you girls need to support her and Ellie and not fight them! I am not one for praying much but I know you all do that a lot! Instead of shouting your wants and needs and should haves. . . I think it would be better to talk to God on this matter. And Alex where are you going?"

"Mr. Braummer that is my mother sitting in that wagon lost and afraid like a scared animal that needs love and kindness. Doc knows I can give that without asking or telling her anything. And my dear sisters can stay away from her for awhile and I mean it!"

As Alex slowly walks to her mother Matt says, "Please girls, please pray for her. Incase you do not know it . . . I love your mother very much . . . and. . ."

"Do not say it Matt . . . I am in no mood!"

"Girls . . . I lost your mother once and I will not loose her again!"

Doc sits down saying, "Great, that is just great . . . is that what I am going to have to listen to from now on?"

Matt sits down next to him saying, "Sounds about right. But if you get her fixed I will not have to say those words again."

"It is not that simple." Doc says sadly. "It is just not that simple. I cannot fix anything. Her body has to do that. We must be patient."

"Just do your best. Looks like that is what Alex is going to do." Matt said sadly as he is given more coffee he sits down struggling to deal with this new situation of Greta and watches Alex slowly walk to her mother and care for her.

Evening came and Greta was still the same. Matt sat with Tom, Brave Eagle, Doc, and MacGhie around the fire discussing the distance to the Pawnee Village and Fort William when the night guard shouts out, "Riders Coming!"

All eyes were looking in the direction of the night guard.

MacGhie shouts, "How many?"

"Looks like two."

"Stand guard." MacGhie says as he stands up with the others.

"Hello in the camp! May we enter?"

"What be your business?" MacGhie shouts.

"Sir we are in search of one Matthew Braummer. We were sent by Minton and Able to retrieve him home."

Matt hears this and says, "Let them in MacGhie."

"You may enter into our camp and are welcome." The men dismount and walk their horses in saying, "Sir do you know the location of Matthew Braummer of Whispering Oaks?"

"I am Matthew Braummer. What is your business with me?"

"Your sister, Emily, has been seriously injured."

Matt stands on the other side of the fire and says, "Come closer to the fire. Do I know you two? And what is this about my sister?"

"We are the brothers of Mrs. Lilly Duvos, wife of Alistair Duvos of Magnolia Cove Plantation next to yours. I am Edward Amonett and my brother Clint. They have sent us to find you. We are to bring you back with us."

Matt smiles and puts forth his hand in friendship saying, "Yes, yes, Edward, Clint, you are welcome. Come sit down by the fire and tell me what reason do you come so far? Wait you said something about my sister."

Reluctantly Edward says, "Yes Sir. Mr. Hadley. . . Sire, he took a whip to your sister."

"What!" Matt stood up quick. "He took a whip to my Emily!"

"Yes Sir . . . Minton saw it all. Said they argued, then when Miss Emily turned to enter her home Mr. Hadley drew his whip in rage and laid it across her back about five times. After Hadley left, Minton helped her into the house. He did not know she saw or heard the whole argument."

Matt was beside himself. He began to pace as Doc tried to reason with him. "Matthew . . . settle down and think this out first."

As Matt continues to pace and looking at the ground he says, "Think Doc. Yes, I will think . . . I will think of the warning I gave him before I left. I will think of my helpless sister attacked by this greedy mad man . . . I will think of his whip and my Emily's back . . . I will think of all that on the way to Louisiana. I will remind Hadley of his dirty deed before I drop him dead!"

Doc grabs his arm saying, "No Matthew! You can not kill him!"

Matt stops and stares into the eyes of his dear friend, "Yes I can . . . it is the code . . . the family code to avenge when one is injured or killed. I will avenge my sister's honor and I will kill Hadley!"

Doc grabs Matt's arm again and says, "My God Matthew . . . do you realize what you are saying? Let the Law take care of him. Do not do this. What about Greta?"

"Do not bring her name up! Do not say her name Doc! She has nothing to do with this! In fact . . . right now . . . she does not even know who I am! So why should I think of her."

"Yes, yes alright then I am going with you!" Doc turns to start gathering the necessary items.

"No Doc. I go alone this time. You have Greta to care for. She needs you not me; I am of no help to her. I am more of a hindrance. Do not worry Doc, I will return once my job is done."

Emma and Ruth walk up with Matt's horse saddled and ready to go. Ruth had food packed for a few days.

Emma hands over the reins to Matt saying, "Mr. Braummer, we understand what you must do and we will pray you make the right decisions. Mother will be all right. Take care of your sister Sir and come back to us safely."

He accepts the reins and the food and says, "Thank you. You are good girls. See you when I see you." Matt gives them each a hug and kiss on their foreheads. He mounts up and leaves with Edward and Clint. Doc watches him and is sad of what he plans to do and wished he could have gone with his friend. Thinking how many miles they can travel before morning comes, Emma breaks his thoughts . . . "I am sure when he gets there he will realize that he should not go through with his avenging plan."

Doc gives Emma a hug saying, "I certainly hope you are right."

Matt, Edward, and Clint traveled by moon light for about ten miles then clouds rolled in and they bedded down in a cold camp. Sleep was only a few hours and they were off before dawn. Travel was fast paced at about twenty-five to thirty miles per day. They arrived at Little Blue River and followed the trail southeast.

"Matt, Edward, look to the west. See the dust rising?"

"Yes. That means a lot of riders." Matt said.

"Good thing they are not coming our way." Edward spoke with a smile.

Matt spoke as he watched the dust in the distance, "I have been thinking. Out here, a campfire is seen for miles. We had better continue with a cold camp. At least until we are out of Indian Country."

The men agreed.

A few nights they had a huge full moon in a cloudless sky giving them a chance to travel farther and close the gap. They would bed down for a few hours giving the horses a rest, then off again closing the gap to their destination.

They finally reached Independence, Missouri. Nine days of cold camps and long hard traveling. They decided to stay one night in a Tavern giving their horses and themselves a good rest. During breakfast, Matt heard some riders talking about making better time on their horse than their friends did on the Steamboat. Matt told that to Edward, and Clint, the decision was made to travel by horseback to San Louie then they would take a Steamboat to

New Orleans. During this time Edward and Clint told Matt what had transpired up until the time they left to find him. Matt was happy to hear how many men came to the aid of his sister. Then he thought of Emily, what Hadley had done and the anger and revenge burned deeper. As they continue on, Matt's thoughts are constant, 'I can not believe this has happened to my sister. How dare Hadley use his whip on my sister . . . oh I know what the Bible says, Vengeance is mine sayeth the Lord; but God, I cannot wait for you to take your vengeance out on him. I burn with anger too much . . . you have to understand my family code . . . you have a code, right God. You follow that code. And Doc telling me to let the Law handle it. Might as well let you do it . . . both will take just as long. I think my way is swifter and no waiting.' . . . his arguing continues in his mind as they pushed to close the distance.

After two weeks on horseback, they arrive in San Louie, boarded a Steamship to New Orleans. The exhausted men now rest on the way to New Orleans. Then back on their horses for two days ride to Whispering Oaks Plantation.

CHAPTER THIRTEEN

The group are now approaching the Pawnee Indian camp. The girls are in awe of the huge village they were coming to.

"Ellie . . . are we safe?" Emma questioned looking at the vast group of Pawnee Indians coming to greet them.

Ellie looked at Mr. MacGhie saying, "Are we safe Mr. MacGhie?"

"Yes." He said with confidence but in his heart he wanted so hard to believe it.

Relieved herself Ellie said, "There is your answer. Satisfied?"

"Yes. Look at them Ellie. How large and with such athletic forms. . . "

"Yes. A dignified countenance is shown. Do you see it?" Ellie said not wanting to point.

"Indeed. Quite different from the Otoes." Emma commented.

"Alright ladies just keep riding. We will camp a few miles away from their village . . . or maybe not. . . "

A band of Pawnee rode fast in front of the group and began talking about the women. Their women were excited to look upon them because there were so many who were white. The Pawnee women have only seen two white women. MacGhie informed the Pawnee that they must push ahead before the snows come to the mountains. It was agreed and the Indians let them pass but not before a number of women walked around the girls and the wagons looking at many items but taking none. Then Greta, Ellie and the girls noted that the village was set up in four huge separate sections and not all together as they would have thought. The Pawnee stared at the girls as much as the girls stared at the stately Indians. At one point, Tom rode up telling them to show no fear, that the Pawnee would rather trade than fight. Katie wondered how to look unafraid and decided to climb into a wagon so she did not see them and they did not see her and she could forget about 'show no fear'.

Making camp was just for over night and they pressed on. Distance wanted to be made between them and the Pawnee. Since they were traveling on the north side of the Platte River MacGhie found a spot to cross the river then on to the South Platte River to cross. At the crossing point it was about two feet deep and a mile wide. Tom said there were times it was two miles wide. And if you did not find the right crossing you could meet up with quicksand. MacGhie knew the right area for crossing.

Close to half way between the forks, the group came to a very steep upgrade. They had a climb of 240 feet in just over one and a half miles they traveled the 18 miles across the high tableland between the South and North Platte rivers before descending Windlass Hill into the North Platte Valley through Ash Hollow. They then traveled the high tableland that became rather a nerve-testing adventure; the only path being along a ridge with a descending slope having a hazardous overhang on each side and it was so narrow that you could not walk along side your lead horse or wagon. This ridge went for about four miles before arriving at the area of descend. In the four miles, not a voice was heard. Everyone concentrated on this sensation of impending danger, at some places the trail was so edge-like that some became a bit giddy.

At the spot of descending, after taking in the area, Katie thought, 'How do we get down?' The other girls questioned the same in their minds. Ellie looked at Greta and asked, "Are you alright?"

"Yes. This area does look familiar. I have been here before and it . . . oh if only I could remember more of who I am and what I am doing out here. Will you please tell me? Perhaps as you tell me things my mind will remember."

"I think you are right Greta. Is there any where you want me to start first?"

"Yes. Those girls. I do know them right?"

"Yes you do. They are your daughters. However, I will introduce you to them later. Right now let me start at the beginning. . . Earleysburg, Pennsylvania. . ." So Ellie sat telling Greta all about her life and about Seth while preparation of lowering wagons, animals and people took place.

MacGhie said, "Alright men . . . get the ropes and the windlass and let's get these wagons and animals down that hill."

First, the wheels were locked by the brake and then tied in place as to not roll. The girls unhitched the horses from each wagon and led them to one side. Ropes were thrown down the hill for the girls to climb down. The descend was roughly 300 feet at a 25 degree slope. Once down they waited for their mother, wagons, animals, and men. Greta was able to climb down, as was Ellie. At the bottom . . . at Ash Hollow, Greta met her daughters for the first time in weeks. It was somewhat awkward as the girls who knew their mother asked to hug her and Greta not knowing the girls accepted their hugs while struggling to remember each of them. The girls were delighted to hear all the birds singing. They began pointing out the beautiful roses and jasmine flowers that were in full bloom and grapes in abundance. A most welcoming place with shade and cool clear water. The girls and men began to hitch up the horses to move the wagons and make camp.

Ellie spoke, "Greta you are still looking around."

"Yes. I know I have been here before and I knew the name Seth meant something to me. However, as far as Mr. Braummer goes . . . I do not recall anything of him."

Ellie was saddened by that piece of news and was at the same time glad Matt was not here. "Will you be alright for awhile Greta? I want to make a fire and get some coffee going for everyone."

"Of course go right ahead. I will just sit here and ponder my thoughts. Ellie, thank you for introducing my daughters to me. I am sure I will remember them in due time. As with everything you told me. Apparently, Doc is correct. We will just have to wait for me to heal."

Greta turns her sites southwest and studies the terrain going deep in her thoughts to an area once thought dead. Thinking to herself, 'We did stop here but we did not continue north . . . we followed the South Platte. We went along at a steady pace . . . oh think, think girl . . . how many days . . . how many . . . we would only stop long enough to eat then on until night fall . . . just short of two weeks . . . ten days . . . eleven days . . . in that direction . . . but it does not make sense. The map said the cabin was northwest of Fort William. We were at a cabin southwest of here. Where did I pack his letter?' her thoughts were broken by Marie saying, "Ma'me! We were calling you and you did not answer. Ellie said the coffee is ready. Please come with us."

"Oh dear, yes let us go. You should have yelled louder." Greta smiled as she walked up to Marie and hugged her saying, "How long will we be staying here?"

"Mr. MacGhie said maybe four days."

"Hum . . . four days." Then whispered 'could be longer.'

"What did you say?"

"I said wish it could be longer. This is such a nice place." Greta looks around the area seeing the birds fly from one tree to another and the flowers; she just loved the beauty they projected.

"How long would you like to stay?"

"Oh I do not know. Maybe two, three weeks."

"Wow that would give us a long rest indeed."

"Indeed it would Marie, indeed it would. Hello girls. Now who made the coffee so when I taste it I can compliment her or teach her how to make it better."

Emma spoke up, "I did Mother. Just the way you taught me." She hands her Mother a cup and Greta tastes it and is pleased, "This is a good cup for sure. So I must be a good teacher at that." Greta paused then said, "Emma. Are there any writing tablets?" Greta said as she sat down on the log.

"Yes Mother. They are in the trunk on top of the quilts. Why?"

"I think I will do some writing this afternoon."

Talk continued about a wide variety of subjects and with everyone preoccupied Greta slips away to the wagon and begins to look for the letter Seth sent before he died. Quickly she went through boxes and trunks until she finally found it. Greta looks outside to see if anyone was coming and they were all still preoccupied so she sat down, opened the letter, and began to read:

'My Dearest Greta,

Long have I wished to see your fair face, sparkling blue eyes, and warm smile to welcome me. Nevertheless my dear, that will have to wait a while longer. I have sent you this money to set aside for our trip to the Cabin in the northwest. The cabin which near sets between the two former Rendezvous of Popo Agie and Wind River. Once at the Fort the area is well known and you will not have difficulty in your travel there.'

"What!" She stops reading and rereads the sentence — *'Once at the Fort the area is well known and you will not have difficulty in your travel there.'* She thinks, 'He did not plan on coming home to take us there!" Then she continues reading on, *'I must stop the writing now and send this to you. Be strong my dearest and trust God. Your husband, Seth.'*

"Oh why did I not see that? He did not intend to take us. But that is not the cabin we first went to. I only knew of the two we were at. One cabin was further north than the first cabin we were at. But not that far north—oh where is that tablet and pencil—there it is—now from Ash Hollow we traveled southwest along the South Platte River on the north side then crossed it following it on the south side then turned west to the cabin—ten days total I think. I can do it in that time. I can get by with a minimum amount of food. No packhorse just Tilly and Tabby. Tabby can carry the food and shelter.' I will ride Tilly. Folding up the paper, she put it in her pocket and the letter in the trunk. Grabbing the old receipt bag, looking at it Greta remembered the time when Seth made it for her, she then quickly emptied it out and put in the necessary items . . . coffee beans, small grinder, a tea block, small coffee pot, small pan with lid, cup, plate, large spoon, flint. She then filled a hunting pouch with items for the Hawken rifle, large measure of powder, extra flint, patching material, patch knife, screwdriver. Gathering up the powder horn and filling it with powder. The possibles sack held the fire-starting kit, eating utensils, and pocketknife. She sets it all under the quilt she sits on. Greta then looks to see where Tom was sitting, as she approaches the fire Tom stands and passes Greta a cup of coffee she takes it asks, "Tom, do Indian women were leggings?"

"Yes some do. Just like these I am wearing. Makes sense too being in the brush and forest; branches can tear up the skin something fierce. Not to mention the ladies skirts."

"I see and just to refresh my memory when you set up a tent covering for the night . . . in which direction would you set it?"

"Well, what I do is look for the direction of broken branches or trees . . . that will tell me the direction the storms come and I put my back to it. Why the questions Mrs. Yancey?"

"Oh Tom. I am just testing my memory to see if it is good. I want you to ask me these questions the next time you see me and that will tell me my memory is growing stronger."

"That sounds pretty good Mrs. Yancey and yes Ma'am the next time I see you I will ask you the same questions you asked me."

"Thank you. This coffee is good."

"Sit a spell then Mrs. Yancey and enjoy it."

"I will do just that." She smiles and sits down. She studies his camp and what he is wearing. Brave Eagle comes into camp and sits down saying, "Evening Ma'am."

She smiles and says, "Why Brave Eagle. You are starting to sound like Tom here."

"Yes Ma'am he helps me much."

"That is good. But why?"

He looks at Tom and Tom says, "Go ahead. You can tell her."

"Yes do tell me why."

"Girl."

"Girl?"

"Yes."

"Who? Which girl?"

"One you call Ruth."

"Oh I see. Ruth. Does she fancy you?" Greta says with a little smile.

"What mean fancy you?" Brave Eagle said looking puzzled.

"Oh I am sorry. Does she like you too?"

"Not sure."

"I see. Well you keep learning what it is you wish to learn and make sure you find out if Ruth likes you too."

"Yes Ma'am. I will."

Greta smiles at Tom then at Brave Eagle but continues to study their campsite.

After awhile Greta excuses herself and takes a walk to the horses. Brave Eagle went to see what Ruth was up to . . . from a distance.

Emma walked up to Tom's campoite and questions "Are the mountains we are going to really larger than our Pennsylvania Mountains?"

"Oh Emma, wait till you see them. Some are so high you would swear God is sitting on 'em just watching over everything He created. There are some Emma, when you climb up them the air is so thin it takes your breath and just that moment you know not to go any further. When it snows, the air is so crisp and fresh. The pines hang low, heavy with snow that a horse cannot walk under. Oh Emma, the water is so good and cold it feels like it could freeze your inners on the spot. Then comes spring and summer then fall, all showing its own colors that God paints for our enjoyment."

"Oh Tom it sounds so beautiful and yet frightening." Emma says.

"Na, not frightening at all. It is respect. Respect those mountains and never underestimate them or the animals that live in them. Know the signs and live. Ignore the signs and die."

"What about the Indians. How do they live in such weather?"

"They travel to different areas during the winter then back in the summer. The hunters are the ones that must truly brave the weather. They leave their village to look for food. In fact that is how Brave Eagle and I met."

"Is that so? Do tell me." Emma sits up eager to listen.

"Well . . . we were hunting the same area when a snow storm came upon us sudden like. The wind was bad. I quickly began to make a snow cave, crawled in, and lit my candle, then waited out the storm. When it finally passed, I had about a foot of snow to break through and when I poked my head out right next to me the head of an Indian poked out of another hole. Come to find out our snow caves were side by side and we did not even know it. We have been together ever since. Guess we figured surviving so close meant something bigger than the both of us did. Been together a long time."

"How exciting Tom. Brave Eagle is a very good man."

"That he is. Saved my life many a time."

"And I am sure you saved his also many a times."

"Yes we both did. Kind of like your Paw and mine. Looking out for each others back."

"Tom . . . do you ever think of your Father?"

"Sure I do. Miss him a lot. What about you?"

"Yes I miss my Father a great deal. He and I became good friends after awhile."

"Not me and my Paw. He always expected too much of me and I never knew how much to give. I just did not measure up to his expectations."

Emma put her hand on his shoulder and said, "Oh Tom. A father always has high expectations for his son. That is only natural."

"Maybe so but I never felt I was good enough for him."

"Did you ever think maybe he never felt good enough for you? Other fathers could give their sons far more than he could ever give you. I remember him, your father, he was a hard man, but he only wanted the best for you. He wanted you to be better than him. He just did not know how to get it across to you. However, he never stopped loving you . . . you were his pride and joy . . . his son that he was so very proud of. I remember when you would play your fiddle and he would just beam with joy . . . he never learned how to play one did he?"

"No. He never did. He wanted to learn in a bad way how to make music but nope never did."

"But you did and he admired you for it. His pride just got in the way of him telling you so. Nevertheless, he did love you . . . his son . . . with all his heart. Do not ever forget that and he knew you loved him."

Tom nodded his head yes and Emma gave him a hug and they quietly sat there for a while looking into the

flame and remembering the good times and the love that
was shared. Emma then excused herself and went back to
her tent.

As Greta is petting Tilly and Tabby, she began to walk
away and they follow her to the first wagon where her
saddle was. She then walks back to the animals and back
to the wagon. No one is paying attention as she grabs the
packed bags and rifle taking them to the area of her saddle. She then walks back to the animals and to the campfire.

"Mother where were you?" Emma questions.

"Oh I was drinking coffee and visiting with Tom."

"Tom? Why?"

"Just wanted to. What do you girls think of Brave Eagle?"

"Oh Mama. He is really interesting." Claire says.

"Yes very nice." Says Marie.

"What about you Ruth?"

The girls giggle and Ruth motions for them to be quiet.

Greta looks at the girls giggling and asks, "What is
funny?"

"I will tell you Mother." Emma begins.

"No. I will tell Mama. They are giggling because I like
him and my sisters continue to tease me about it." Ruth
says.

Greta smiles then says, "I suggest you stop the teasing.
Remember . . . what goes around comes around. Moreover,
it is nice that you like Brave Eagle. Does he like you also?"

"I am not sure Mama. We do not talk to each other. We
only smile at one another."

"I see." Greta says then continues, "Well then girls
what are you planning to do after supper?"

Emma spoke first, "Since we will be here a few days
we set up the small tents and I plan on doing a lot of reading."

Anne said, "I was thinking on doing some sewing if
Marie will read out loud to me."

"Yes I will read. One of the men lent me his book of stories and I have been wanting to read it. So I will read to you Anne."

"Sounds very nice."

"What about you Mother? What will you do?" Emma questions.

"You know, I think I will just crawl under the wagon and enjoy the night air. If it gets chilly I will crawl into the wagon."

"Ellie what about you?" Questions Greta.

"I am going right to sleep in my tent." She says smiling.

"Well then when we finish our coffee I will see you come morning." Greta says.

"We decided to take our second cup with us and get an early start on relaxing."

The girls fill their cups and Emma says, "That sounds like a good idea. You go on and I will finish my second cup in the wagon. And an early good night girls, sleep tight and no worrying, things will be fine."

"I too am taking my cup to my tent and totally relaxing." Ellie says.

"Good night Ellie."

Doc walks up to the camp just as Ellie enters her tent.

"Good evening Greta."

"Evening Doc. Have a cup of coffee."

"Thank you."

"Why are the girls turning in now? It is still early."

"They want to get some good reading and relaxing in while we are here a few days."

"That does sound like a great idea."

"Yes it does Doc."

"Where is your tent Greta?"

"My tent? Oh I am sleeping under the wagon unless it gets too chilly then I will sleep in the wagon." She points to the wagon she will lay under.

"Looks like a full moon tonight." Doc says looking up.

Greta agrees and thinks, 'just right for traveling.'

Doc excuses himself saying it is time for his relaxing.

As time goes on Greta pays close attention to the camp of Tom Cooper and Brave Eagle. She thinks 'I should know enough about the wilderness life to get by after all I did live that life for awhile.' Greta lies under the wagon and watches everyone entering their tents for the night. She then adds more bedding in her quilt to make it look like someone is sleeping; she then slowly removes the rifle from the wagon quietly walking to her horses. Greta ties cloth around the feet of Tabby her packhorse and around Tilly, the one she will ride. She then ties down the packs and leads them slowly away from camp being cautious to keep the trees between her and the wagons. The moon lit the way for her as she continues to slowly walk the horses. She was happy to know that Sergeant was in the tent with Emma so no sound from him to stir the others. Greta walked the horses about a mile then mounted up and after crossing the South Platte; she followed the river in a southwestern direction. About three hours into the night, she dismounted and unpacked the pair of leggings and shirt that belonged to Tom. She had a time getting them from him as to not arouse his curiosity . . . she told him Anne could put in an extra row of thread for sturdiness and he agreed knowing full well he would have no trouble doing it himself. He figured he would let the girl do it and make her happy.

As Greta changed, she listened intently to the sounds around her. Getting familiar with the natural noises. Thinking, 'oh good these leggings are comfortable and the shirt is big but it will do. She then slipped on the powder horn, belt of necessities, knife, and hatchet and finally a hat she found in Docs tent. She mounted Tilly and continued to follow the river staying in the shadows as best as she could. Come morning she could pick up the pace.

CHAPTER FOURTEEN

Minton, standing by the table rubbing one foot on top the other was cutting up vegetables and dropping them in a large iron kettle while also paying attention to the bread baking when she heard men saying riders were approaching. She goes to the front to see Edward, Clint, and Matthew ride up.

Matthew jumped from his horse before it stopped and ran up the stairs in the front door giving Minton a hug and turned to Alistair saying, "Alistair, good to see you." Shaking hands Alistair said, "Yes it is good to see you also Matthew. Emily is upstairs. She is very weak."

Matthew looks to the stairs then says, "Thank you very much Alistair for all your help."

"We are here for as long as you need us, Matthew. We have worked out a great plan to keep your home and the rest of the homes safe."

Patting him on the shoulder Matthew goes to the stairs saying, "I must see Emily first. Then we will talk."

Alistair nods and watches him run up the stairs, taking two stairs at a time.

He enters Emily's room slightly startling Violet and Lilly who were just changing the bandages and Matthew saw the full back of lash marks. He looks at the two women saying, "Anyone else injured?"

"No Matthew, just Emily . . . I am so sorry." Lilly says with sadden eyes.

He looks again at his sisters back then says, "Thank you both for all you are doing. Will she live?

Lilly answers, "Why yes of course she will live. Emily is strong and—"

Matthew interrupts saying, "I will return."

Alistair waited at the bottom of the stairs to continue talking but Matthew walked by him saying, "When I return we will talk more. Right now I have something to do." Matthew's strides were long and filled full of determination and authority as he walked out of the house mounted his horse and left.

"Where is he going?" Clint questioned.

"To the man who injured his sister, I would suspect." Alistair says.

"Alone?"

"Yes alone. Come, you must be tired. Minton! Coffee please." Alistair says as he points the way to the dining room.

As Matthew rode hard to get to Hadley's home his thoughts were of his sister and the image of the wounds this man created on Emily's back were burned in his mind. As he approaches the plantation, he could see no one was around. Matt thinks . . . 'they must be out in the fields or heading to Emily.' He dismounts at the porch and enters into Hadley's home finding him alone in the Library.

Half-laughing Hadley says, "You are a fool Matthew Braummer! You are a fool to think you could stand there aiming that pistol at me and think I would come to be in fear. And Alistair Duvos with his brothers and his wife's brothers thinking they could stop me with all the other Plantation owners!"

With no expression on his face Matthew says, "They did stop you."

Again half-laughing, he leans back from his desk saying, "Oh they thought they stopped me. So did your parents. I will have Whispering Oaks even if it takes killing the rest of the Braummer family. . . "

"You had my brothers and sisters killed!" Matthews eyes grew larger and his body tensed.

"Yes of course . . . you mean you did not put it all together (laughing), I would have killed Emily too if I could have found her. Your parents still would not sell because of you and Emily. My terms are clear. Emily will marry my son and you will sign Whispering Oaks over to me!"

Matthew tightens his grip on the pistol saying, "No Sir! Today . . . you will die and there is not a man in all of Louisiana nor in this Country that would begrudge me for what I am about to do."

"Strong words from a son of a coward." Laughing he continues, "Your father stood in the very same place you stand in many years ago and said the same thing, then could not do it . . . and left . . . as you will also leave. You are your father's son. I will watch you turn and leave, now!"

"You forget Sir. I am also my Mother's Son!"

"Aaa yes . . . I did forget. Your mother, yes, she was once called the daughter of a wench. Your mother, excuse me for laughing, was the granddaughter of Pirate Mary Read. Am I to fear you because of your Great Grandmother?" He laughs even more. Matthew watches as Hadley's belly, and fat face shakes.

Matthew then says, "No . . . you fear me because I am Matthew William Braummer, the owner of Whispering Oaks avenging my family's killings and my sisters beating. You fear me because a Pirates blood runs thick in me not just from Mary Read but from Pirate Captain William Fly."

"What?"

"Do not look so surprised . . . it is apparent my father did not want to become his Father. Therefore, he walked away. My blood is Pirate thick and like I said there is not a man in Louisiana nor this Country that would begrudge me for what I am about to do." Matthew William Braummer, not breaking a sweat and with a steady hand raised his pistol.

"Your blood may be a Pirates blood but the years have softened you. . . ."

Showing no emotion Matthew pulled the trigger of his pistol with a steady hand and watched the breath leave the body of fat man Hadley then turned and walked out. He mounted his horse, looking around to see no one in sight then returning to Whispering Oaks and to the side of his sister Emily. He watched her lay there breathing and settled in himself that what he had just completed was for the good of all men in the area . . . not just for Emily. He laid his head next to Emily and asked God if he could ever forgive him for what he had done. He then sat back in the large chair resting his head against the back knowing he could finally fall asleep in peace. When Lilly came into the room and saw Matthew sleeping in the chair she quickly checked Emily and left informing her husband and brothers to let Matthew sleep.

Morning came and Alistair gives Matthew a couple nudges to wake him.

"Good morning Matthew." Alistair says smiling.

"Good morning Alistair." He looks at his sister who is moving. Matt leans toward her saying, "Emily. Emily. It is I Matt. I am here and you have nothing to worry about any more. Just get well."

Quietly Emily says, "Matt. Is that really you or am I dreaming?"

"Yes dear Emily it is your brother Matthew." He says as he moves her hair from her face.

She tries to roll on her back but cannot.

"Emily just lay there. You are in no condition to get up."

"Oh Matt. I must. Mr. Hadley said he would be back in the morning and take me to marry Owen. I must not let him in."

"No need to worry about that. He will not be coming here anymore."

"Oh. How can you be so sure Matt?" Emily's eyes fill with tears as she spoke. "How can you be?"

"I can be very sure. Trust me my dear Emily. Now just rest."

With that, she said no more and fell back asleep. Matt walks downstairs with Alistair to the kitchen where coffee is waiting for them.

"You boyz jest sit down 'n breakfast will be soon on da table."

"Thank you Minton."

"Oh Mista Matthew is shore is good to have you home. Will you be staying long?"

"As long as needed Minton."

"Dat shore sounds good. But wat 'bout yoz new wife to be. Aint she gonna be mad wif you?" Minton says with her hands on her hips.

"No Minton. Not at all. We are not married yet."

Surprised she said, "Not married. Wats wrong wif dat girl. She got no good sense at all."

"That is alright Minton. Do not worry about that but, please do worry about our breakfast. I am famished!" He slaps Alistair on the arm and says, "You famished Alistair . . . tell Minton." They both laugh.

"Oh Mista Matthew I do it rite now for you men." She turns and laughs as she prepares the biscuits and gravy.

CHAPTER FIFTEEN

Five in the morning and the sun was just breaking the horizon and Ellie was up starting a fire as everyone else slowly woke. No one was in a hurry and only the absolute necessary things of the day were being done. Soon it was breakfast and time to call the last one to eat, Greta. They all took turns calling her and finally, Ellie said, "Someone just go wake your mother up. Please. My my, she must have really needed that sleep."

Katie said, "I will go wake her."

Emma said, "For Mother it must have felt good to sleep on something solid as the ground."

Claire said, "Just think of Mama in the wagon all that time. It had to be uncomfortable."

"Yes but Mama did not complain." Marie said.

Suddenly Katie yells, "Ellie! Mama is not here!"

"What!"

They all run to the wagon to find only bedding. With one question, "Where is she?"

Ellie yells, "Tom! Doc! Come quick!"

They come running along with Mr. MacGhie and Brave Eagle and a few other men.

Katie said, "I went to wake my mother up and all I found was this bedding rolled up in her quilt."

"Did you look in the wagon?" Doc questioned.

Emma jumps up on the back and looks in saying, "She is not here, but she sure was. Things are moved all around in here."

"All right now just calm down and do some serious thinking. Ellie how is the coffee doing?"

"Coffee is done Doc."

"Good. Let's go have coffee, finish waking up and talk about this."

They walk to the fire and Brave Eagle says to Tom, "I look you go there listen."

"Right."

Doc begins by questioning when was the last time anyone saw her, and says, "I think I was the last one who saw her. We had coffee together just after the girls went into their tents. We talked about the full moon. Yes and she said she was lying under the wagon pointing to that one. Also, that it would be a good night for traveling. I then was thinking about her laying under the wagon and I thought how wonderful that sounded so I did the same thing and fell fast asleep."

"Did anyone see or hear anything?" MacGhie asked.

Tom spoke, "Mrs. Yancey spent some time with Brave Eagle and I. Of course I did not think anything of it."

"And now?"

"I am not sure."

"Tell us what she talked about."

The girls were sitting and hanging on every word that Tom spoke as Ellie unwrapped the spice cake to cut and hand out.

"Let me think now. She asked if Indian women wore leggings and wanted her memory refreshed about the set up of a tent covering for the night. She asked in which direction to set one up. I asked her why the questions; she said she was just testing her memory to see if it was good and wanted me to question her on this the next time I saw her. I did not think anything of it."

Anne questions, "Then mother was testing herself . . . that does not sound unusual after loosing her memory."

Claire then says, "That is, if mother was testing her memory, or was she after information for some other reason. Because she is gone."

"Maybe she just went for a walk." Katie said.

Marie got up and ran to the wagon and Claire was hot on her heals; they climbed in and began looking around. Claire said, "We were thinking the same thing Marie . . . the Hawkins is gone."

"And the receipts are in this trunk loose. No receipt bag. What did Father use that for?" Marie questions.

"Items one would use daily, like coffee beans, tea block, and such. The powder horn is also gone."

"And look here . . . food is missing."

Brave Eagle looks in the wagon, "You right. Mother go far. Take two horses. Come we tell others. Say nothing about two horses."

Claire and Marie look at Brave Eagle and Marie says, "I was hoping Mama was just testing us but she is not."

Claire said, "She really left."

"Yes. Test is where she go. Come now."

They run back to camp saying what is missing and what Brave Eagle said.

Talk began to clutter the air and MacGhie quieted them down.

Tom asked, "Anne, did your mother give you my shirt and leggings to sew an extra stitch in?"

"No she did not."

He looks at Brave Eagle then says; "Now everyone sit down and be very quiet and think of yesterday. Think only of Greta and what was said by her and to her." He explained about the leggings and shirt and how she was studying their campsite. Which neither Tom nor Brave Eagle thought unusual.

More small talk until Ellie said, "Wait a minute. When we arrived here at Ash Hallow, Greta was acting very peculiar. She said she has been here before and it was not on the map Seth gave her. I mentioned that it was too bad the map blew away and she said 'it may be physically gone but it is very clear in my memory.' She said she would take a ride in that direction but first we set up camp."

Marie said, "Mother kept looking around and when I asked about it she said she was just remembering, said something about a cabin and Father."

Katie stood up, "Remember when we were calling for Mama to eat. She came and questioned how long Mr. MacGhie said we would stay. Ellie said four days and I know mother said she wished it could be longer . . . two weeks longer giving a good rest. Then she asked Emma about the writing tablets."

"Now I speak. Mother leave with two horses, put cloth over feet to quiet sounds, she walk horses in that direction." He points toward the south river.

Everyone followed Brave Eagles finger in the directing it was pointing.

MacGhie said, "Southwest! Now why southwest?"

Ruth, Claire, and Marie said together, "A cabin."

Ellie says, "What cabin?"

Tom says, "Check what is missing. That will give us an idea of what she took and how long she will be gone."

Ellie said again, "What cabin?"

Brave Eagle said, "Aaaa, Mrs. Yancey smart. She take moccasins I make sister."

Tom whispers to Brave Eagle, "Sure hope she thought of Indians."

"Ssssh, no tell them. They go crazy."

"I believe you are right." Tom said as both men looked at the group.

CHAPTER SIXTEEN

During breakfast Alistair says, "Well Matthew. I suppose you will be heading north soon and back to your bride to be."

"No, not yet. I want to make sure Emily is fully recovered before leaving."

"You know there is no need for that. There are enough folks around here to care for her and Whispering Oaks . . . now that Hadley will not be a bother anymore. He will not be . . . correct Matthew?"

"You can be sure of that. I just want to see my sister in better condition than she is right now."

As soon as your sister realizes Hadley will no longer be a problem she will recover fast. And you did say he will not be a problem."

"I did say that and Alistair, when you hear from others that Hadley will not be a problem . . . say nothing to them about me."

"But Matthew. We all know you went there."

"You all know I left the plantation but you do not know where I went."

"True. We do not know. But is it safe for you to stay here for a long period of time?"

Matthew smiles, "Alistair, you have always been to smart for your own good. It could be a little dangerous for me. And my friend . . . when my horse is gone, I will be gone. No one will know therefore no one can answer."

Both men smile in agreement and Alistair says, "Do not worry about Emily. Guard yourself closely."

"I will Alistair, I will. Minton, more coffee please."

"Comin' wif it now Sir."

Days went by and Emily was getting better. She was able to sit up and show signs of her old self. Though the scars of the brutal man will always be with her the brute himself, will not. Emily had many long talks with Matthew and they grew closer than ever before. However, both knew it would be short lived.

Owen Hadley came once to Whispering Oaks after his Fathers funeral questioning where Matt was on the day his Father was killed. He knew Matt was against everything his Father did especially marrying Emily. Matt stayed calmed in his discussion with Owen as he made his point very clear for Owen or any member of his plantation to never come on this land again. Owen did agree to never show his face on Whispering Oaks again. Nevertheless, he vowed to find the culprit of his fathers killing, though he had not one clue. When Owen left, Matt was sure that would be the last time they would see anyone from the Hadley estate again.

Weeks have gone by and Emily was happy to have Matt home dealing with the works of Whispering Oaks. They delighted in each other sharing thoughts and stories long over due. Both with the understanding that Matt will one day have to leave.

Lilly entered Emily's room and saw her standing in front of the large open doors to her balcony as the long white drapes blew about her in the morning breeze.

"Emily, should you be out of bed and in front of that door . . . you will catch your death . . . what are you looking at."

"Lilly, I am much stronger than ever and I must continue to grow stronger and healthier if I am to attend my brothers wedding. You know it will be a long hard ride to where they will live."

Lilly laughed saying, "Your brother? Married? With all do respect my dear friend . . . he will stay here and continue to run Whispering Oaks. I do not see him ever marrying. There is something mysterious about him that will always stop him."

"I do not think so Lilly. He will marry."

Lilly laughs again saying, "Dear Emily, how can you be so sure? I love you both very much and want only the best for the both of you. Nevertheless, Matthew will not marry. He has been free to long of a time to submit to wedding vows."

Emily turns smiling and says, "Lilly you will soon hear Matthew's horse is gone. You will know then he continues his quest to marry Greta Yancey once and for all."

Lilly looks hard at Emily then at the open doorway to the balcony and says, "He did leave?"

Emily smiles and says, "Hours ago."

"Did he say where he was going? Did he truly go west to find Mrs. Yancey?" Lilly questions as she looks out the open doors.

"He only said I am not to worry about him, that he would return and for me to continue healing so that I may attend his wedding."

"Do say. Well I would have never figured Matthew to go through with this wedding."

Emily looks out the open doors, as the sun climbs above the bushes and smiling, knowing her brother will finally be happy.

CHAPTER SEVENTEEN

On the vast open prairie, the morning was bright and sunny as Greta continued following the South Platte River. She talks to her only two companions Tilly and Tabby, "Well old girls, we put some good miles in during the night, we will just take it slow and easy. I am trusting you God, you said to fear not and I will work at keeping all fear away. I am also trusting in your guidance. I will pay attention as you guide me through this land. Thank you God and please restore my memory, those girls are wonderful and I would like to know them as I did before. And who is this Matt character?"

Greta travels along the river keeping a sharp eye out for anything moving other than animals. She covers more miles and more hours. "Looks to be about the noon time now. We will stop just up ahead. You girls could probably use a nice rest."

She dismounts and while the horses drink, she takes a good look around the area. Seeing no traces of Indians, Greta builds a small fire in a little cove and makes some coffee.

"These muffins that girl Ruth made sure are good and later I will have a piece of that spice cake. I hope they do not mind that I took the whole thing. I did see a second one wrapped up and I am sure she will be making more."

Greta rested about an hour then mounted up and headed in the same southwest direction.

"Nice area right girls. Birds singing and that fish I caught a while back tasted good from that little stream. The spice cake complimented it very nice. To bad you girls only eat grass and such. You would find my meals very tasty. Just look at the open land. I remember Seth saying this was Pawnee land and Buffalo. Since we came across that Pawnee village quite a ways back, I do not think there would be another. Nevertheless, Tilly and Tabby, there are other Indians we have to watch out for. I think as long as we stay close to the river we should be all right. Sky looks clear; maybe we will travel a bit at night too. Now how about a good run?"

As she ran, Greta saw other horses' tracks and realized she was behind either a war party or hunting party because the droppings of the horses were scattered. If it were wild horses there would be piles. Wild horses stop to relieve themselves; Indian horses relieve themselves on the run. Greta had no choice but to follow the tracks. She followed them about two hours keeping a keen eye on the areas far ahead of her. The tracks then crossed the river, she decided to run a cold camp this night. Her travel pace will be picked up to make the best time possible without hurting her horses.

CHAPTER EIGHTEEN

"Brave Eagle and I will go after Mrs. Yancey. Are you going to wait or continue on to Fort William?"

MacGhie answered, "We can wait here for a few more days, but then it will be important to get these ladies to the Fort. If you do not return in four days time, know that we are on the move to the Fort. Even if we stay five or six days, you two head to the Fort after four days or after you retrieve Mrs. Yancey."

"We will do that."

"Take care Tom and be careful. You to Brave Eagle."

"Thanks MacGhie, we will." Tom says as they both nod their heads in agreement.

"May I go too Tom?"

"No Emma. We cannot take the chance of you holding us back."

"I would not hold you back—"

"Please Emma, do not argue with me right now. Brave Eagle and I will find her. She cannot be more than a half day ahead of us."

"Do not be so sure of that Tom. Mrs. Yancey is not the same person that started out with us. Her mind has reversed and only remembers things of many years back. Moreover, in that time, she trapped with her husband Seth, was extremely active, and traveled the plains with him. So you must think in terms of following another mountain man. How do you and Brave Eagle travel when you need to get somewhere fast? That is how she will travel and she will not hurt her horses in doing so."

"I understand Mother. The quicker we leave the better the gap we will close."

"I will have the girls pack food for you."

"Thank you Mother. We will leave in one hour."

"Good enough." Ellie said and began giving instructions to Ruth and Emma as she tosses a bag at them to fill.

"Come, we get tents and horses." Brave Eagle said.

Tom agreed and within the hour, they were on the trail in pursuit of Mrs. Yancey. Once they were far enough away from camp Tom says, "My friend I think I know where Mrs. Yancey in heading. Remember years ago we traveled from Seth's cabin going south to the other one he told us about incase we were caught in a storm we could have shelter?"

"Yes."

"That is where she is heading. He only took her there once and he never took her to the one near Popo Agie."

"Why he have many place's?"

"I am not sure. I often wondered that myself. My Father only knew of the two, not this southern one."

"Seth strange man. Like raven, mysteries, and strange."

"That he was."

◆◆◆

Back at Ash Hollow Katie was upset. "Now what do we do? Just wait? I cannot believe this is happening. . . "

"Katie . . . go write in your journal." Ruth said.

"No way. Not this time. I cannot write as fast as I am thinking. What was the purpose for this move I do not see. . ."

"Katie! Not now! It happened and that is that. Mother knows what she is doing."

"Oh really. She barely remembers us so how. . . "

Ellie spoke up, "Katie come with me. Come on, let's walk a little."

"Fine I feel like going after her myself."

"Do you? And where would you look?"

"I would follow the tracks."

"I see. So you can spot trail?"

"Yes I can."

"Look there, what is that?"

"Looks like a bear paw." She pauses and looks around then says, "Are there bear around here?"

"Could be, but, that is no bear paw print."

"No. Then what is it?"

"When the wind would blow, the spears of grass would bend over toward the ground and the oscillating motion would scoop out the loose sand into this shape. Honey, there is more to trailing tracks than even I know."

"Oh. I . . . I guess I am scared Ellie."

"Of course you are. We have had it rough and no telling what is ahead of us. Nevertheless, Katie, please do not go running off trying to find your Mother. Believe me; your mother knows what she is doing. I have every confidence that no harm will come to her. Where ever she went and for whatever reason, she will survive and when she is done will return to us."

"Will Mr. Tom and Brave Eagle find her?"

"Well . . . knowing your Mother she will not make it easy. She knows she is in Indian Country and she knows what to do. Now, what I want you to do and need you to do is continue writing in your journal, which will help you out a great deal."

"Not to mention everyone else. Right?"

"Not to mention . . . but yes."

"Alright Ellie. I will and I will pray for Mother too. I may not be able to say things to God how Mama or Emma do but like Mr. Braummer said God still hears us."

"Mr. Braummer said that did he."

"Yes Ma'am and know what, I am glad he is not here right now. He would be a terrible handful to deal with. He does not write in a journal."

Ellie agrees and they both laugh a little thinking of how Mr. Braummer would be.

"Come on Katie, let's go get some coffee and a piece of spice cake. How does that sound to you?"

"That sounds good."

CHAPTER NINETEEN

Mr. MacGhie, knowing he could not wait a week for Tom and Brave Eagle to return, announced on the fourth day that they were breaking camp and heading out. The group prepared for travel and left early in the morning. The sky was a magnificent blue behind scattered white clouds. The group moved along at a healthy pace. Nearing the afternoon time, a new noise was heard by the ladies.

"Marie, hear that?" Katie questions.

"Yes, what is it?"

"Emma what is that sound?"

"I do not know but it is getting louder." Emma turns to seek out one of the men to question what the sound was when she saw a huge black mass coming in their direction. She shouts, "MacGhie...what do we do?"

"Hold up! Stop that lead wagon! That herd has to be turned or we are dead!"

"Turned?" Emma looks at the great mass of buffalo coming toward them she yells again, "Turned?" She knows in her mind how to turn cattle but a thunderous herd of buffalo is beyond her imagination. Emma shouts to Ellie to hold up as the men begin to shout and wave anything they can to turnthat wave of roaring death coming at them. The Buffalo traveled at a rapid gait, taking the herd two full days to pass. These two days were spent with guards placed around the parameter of the campsite who continued to shout and wave things, then at night, huge bonfires were built to aid in the safety of the group, and the continuing chore of keeping that herd turned.

"Looks like the last of them." MacGhie shouts.

"Oh my God, I have never seen anything so awesome!" Marie said.

"Awesome yes but very deadly." MacGhie said. "We leave in the morning. Build a good fire and the men that got sleep last night stand guard tonight. Thank you ladies for keeping the fires going. I know it was difficult now get some sleep."

The girls get in their tents and Isaac goes in by Alex who says, "That was very frightening Isaac. We were actually scared for you out there with the others shouting and waving as those buffalo went by."

"Yes and now they will watch for Indians. There may be a hunting party. . ." Isaac paused a moment then said, "What did you mean when you said 'we were scared for you' . . . you were alone while your sisters . . . built . . . the . . . fire. . . Oh my God! Alex . . . you are having a baby!"

"Yes!" Alex said with a big smile.

Isaac picks her up and swings her around then carries her out of the tent shouting, "We are having a baby! We are having a baby!"

Ruth comes running shouting to Emma, "Boil water, Alex is having a baby! Get some clean cloths. . ." She continues to shout about the water and blankets while the men are now running here and there. The sisters come running and Ellie says, "When is it due?"

"In the spring."

Everyone stops and Ruth says, "In the spring!"

Marie puts down the bucket and runs to Alex saying, "You are really having a baby Alex? A real baby?"

"Yes I am Marie."

MacGhie says, "Well what do you know. A baby! Congratulations Isaac, Alex! We need to celebrate."

As the men scurry to get their fiddles and harmonicas, others are going up to the happy couple and congratulating them. Isaac was getting a good arm shaking.

The music began and everyone was dancing and having a grand time. Even during this joyous time, their thoughts would drift to think about Matt, Greta, Tom and Brave Eagle, that all will go well for them.

The terrain was now short grass prairie and scrub vegetation. Buttes and other rocky outcrops were scattered through out. The men called it the high plains as they are rising in elevation.

"Look up there Marie, is that the Rocky Mountains?" Katie said excited.

"I do not know. Lets ride over to Ellie and ask her."

The girls rode up pointing in the direction of the mountains saying, "Ellie is that the Rocky Mountains?"

"No, I would say not. Mr. MacGhie, what is that large mountain?"

MacGhie looks and smiles, "That Courthouse Rock and Jail Rock. Also known as old castle. It is about three days ride. Then after that you will see Chimney Rock another days ride after Courthouse Rock. Chimney Rock looks like a chimney. Wait you will see when we get there. Land marks is what they are. There is good water and grass but still no wood. Keep using the buffalo-chips."

"Thank you. Three days ahead. One sure can see a long distance out here." Marie said.

That night at camp the girls were all talking bout the "landmarks" ahead. How the terrain is so different from a month ago. They pray for their mother, Tom and Brave Eagle. Hoping the three are now all together. Emma said it was time for some scripture reading and the girls got more coffee, another slice of Ruth's spice cake and got comfortable for the reading.

Emma opened her Bible and said, "I will continue to read where I left off in the book of First John chapter five verse five *'This then is the message which we have heard of him, and declare unto you, that God is light, and in him is no darkness at all. If we say that we have fellowship with him, and walk in darkness, we lie, and do not the truth: But if we walk in the light, as he is in the light, we have fellowship one with another, and the blood of Jesus Christ his Son cleanseth us from all sin. If we say that we have no sin, we deceive ourselves, and the truth is not in us. If we confess out sins, he is faithful and just to forgive us our sins, and to cleanse us from all unrighteousness. If we say that we have not sinned, we make him a liar, and his word is not in us.'* "Continuing on in Chapter two verse one, *'My little children, these things write I unto you, that ye sin not. And if any man sin, we have an advocate with the Father, Jesus Christ the righteous: And he is the propitiation for our sins: and not for ours only, but also for the sins of the whole world.'* I will continue tomorrow night."

"Emma, what does propitiation mean?" Marie questions.

"It means he, Jesus Christ, is the sacrifice and High Priest sacrificing himself for our sins. Which reconciles us to God. That is why Jesus is called our Savior. The only way to heaven is through Jesus as our Savior."

"Oh, I see now, thank you Emma." Marie says smiling.

"Your welcome. Now let us get to bed. Good night girls."

They say their good nights and off to bed.

They pass Courthouse and Jail Rock and camp near Chimney Rock which indeed looked like a chimney. No wood but a lot of buffalo-chips could be found. A very pleasant place to camp despite all the bad weather and the wind picking up at time to be very extreme. There wasn't a day that went by that storms did were not present at some point in the day. But the day at Chimney Rock proved to be a pleasant one and then they were off again. Still no sign of Tom, Brave Eagle or Greta. MacGhie figured on the trail they would take to get to Fort William but did not share it with the girls. Nor did Doc who spoke a great deal with MacGhie.

Soon the girls saw another huge "mountain" and questioned what it was.

"Emma what is that up ahead?" Marie questioned.

"I do not know. Guess we will just have to wait and see."

Mr. MacGhie road ahead of the wagons for quite a ways then returned to the lead wagon pointing toward the large bluff. He again road ahead of the wagon and marked an area for everyone to stop for the night.

When everyone was settled in the girls were inquiring about this bluff and Mr. MacGhie was glad to answer their questions.

He said, "That is called Scott's Bluff. It is named after a mountain man that was left here to die after his injuries were to great to continue on. You will see yourselves how beautiful this area is and how treacherous."

"We cannot continue on the way we were going? Along side the river?" Ellie asked.

"No the ground between Scott's Bluff and the river are two wet for the wagons to travel over. This will be a hard days work as we go through Robidoux Pass. But we can do it." Mr. MacGhie said. "We will start early in the morning so get a good nights sleep."

Come morning Ellie made breakfast while the girls hitched up the horses and followed the instructions to double check that everything was tied down good and tight.

This time the mules and most of the men took the lead followed by the wagons. Ellie climbed up on the first wagon set herself on the seat grabbed the rains and waited for the shout to move out. Behind her Ruth, Claire, and Issac also climbed up on their wagons and waited. Behind wagons Anne, Katie and Marie on their horses waited to move the cattle, horses and pigs along the unknown trail. There were also about eight men that were with them to give assistance.

They began the move toward this colossal mountain. The group ascended about sixty feet but narrowing, winding, and walled in; the ascent was slight, and it looked like it could be a river-bottom but no time to ask. The group continued winding around through this huge mountain of strange shapes, pillar, dome, spire, just unbelievable. They ascended insensibly mile after mile some thirteen, fourteen miles. Then before they were aware, or hardly knew how, they found themselves riding above and looking into a deep glen, with large trees, cedars, shrubbery, rocks and crystal waters.

Marie says to Katie and Anne "Where is the outlet? We are very high up."

Anne said looking around, "Yes I see that and look at this vast grassy plain."

Katie said, "Did you even realize we were going up? I did not."

Anne said still looking around, "No I never did but look at this area and the tall walls around it. And look up there, trees, those are trees way up there."

Marie looked up then looked straight to the right and said, "Is that berries over there? Katie, Anne, look, those are berries." At that she turned her horse and went in that direction.

Katie and Anne both yelled, "Marie no, stay here! Come back!"

Soon Marie dismounted and began to pick the berries and grapes that were abundant. She cupped her skirt and began filling it.

Leavitt one of the men that was nearest the girls heard them yelling and looked in the direction they were looking.

Marie turned and yelled, "Hurry girls there are lots of good berries here! Come on and help me!" Marie then heard a rustling in the brush just beyond and then before she could move a huge grizzly bear stood up and roared at her. Marie froze in place, she could feel the blood drain from her face as she was scared in place staring at this huge mean animal. The roar alerted everyone and the men closest were already loading guns and shouting and running in her direction. The big grizzly raised his arm and dropped it across Marie's right arm. Marie fell to the ground and did not move. Soon after shots were heard and the grizzly finally dropped to the ground with a loud thud.

Everyone was at Marie's side. Mr. MacGhie and a few of the other men began checking Marie's arm to make sure it was in-tacked. Doc arrived with his bag to continue and MacGhie then assisted Doc. Her arm was severely ripped up from the claws and Doc began sewing her up. He did not want to move her until the larger wounds were sewn. When Isaac told Alex what had happen she instructed him to send Emma and Ruth to help her fix up a spot for Marie. Alex said she will care for her in the wagon. Isaac returned to the area where everyone was at and told Emma and Ruth what Alex had said.

Emma saw that her sisters Katie and Anne were still stunned over the whole ordeal and she shouted to Katie and Anne, "Come with us girls, you can give a hand at Alex's wagon."

They did not hesitate in leaving that area. They knew Marie was in good hands and they heard the men making plans on keeping watch during the night and building high fires. Where there is one grizzly there may be another.

When Doc was done he watched as Leavitt picked Marie up and carried her to the wagon. Lifting her up the girls were there to grab her and set her on the quilts. Doc instructed to watch for fever.

MacGhie said, "We can stay on top this plane for a day but then we have to get off it. We do not need to be up here in a storm."

The men took care of the grizzly bear and began work on the hide. Others cut up the meat. Leavitt stayed close to Alex's wagon with gun loaded and stood watch all night.

At one time during the night Marie woke up and Alex spoke with her. She was hurt extremely but did not feel feverish or sick. Alex gave her some biscuits to eat and water to drink and she did just fine. Leavitt spoke with her for awhile then excused himself to continue his watch.

MacGhie walked over to the wagon when he saw the light and when he found out Marie was doing much better he said they could leave in the late morning.

In the morning Ellie had breakfast going. Katie and Anne walked over to Marie with a bowl of berries for her and though she was grateful. She was a little reluctant to eat them after what she went through because of the berries. But she did eat them and her sisters were happy to see how well she was doing.

After breakfast everyone once again took their places to leave.

At one certain bend in the road they were on top of the mountain gap with an almost boundless view, on their right to which they must now direct their course, far below and about twelve miles off, were the grassy meadows of Horse Creek; beyond that its blue hills. Then, farther away above many treeless hills and plain rose the view of the Black Hills and Laramie Mountain. MacGhie said their highest peak towering at eighty miles. MacGhie waited for everyone to see this magnificent view then they turned to descend another plain of twelve miles turning southwest. They came upon Horse Creek and stayed the night near its mouth. It resembled the Platte but the water was clearer.

In the morning they continued to descend crossing gravelly hills until they came to the Platte River once again and there camped the night. Then onward to Fort William.

CHAPTER TWENTY

From the flat lands, Greta gradually ascends westward up to mountain country. As she travels she notices the mornings and evenings are cooler than usual. The area began to look familiar and this night she did not run a cold camp. Come morning she mounted up and continued onward.

It was early afternoon when Greta ties Tabby to a tree and rides Tilly up the hill. She thinks, "Just how I envisioned it; smoke billowing out of the chimney and the cabin nestled among tall pines. Hum . . . one horse just grazing, someone must be home.' Greta dismounts walks up to the cabin door and knocks on it, not sure of who is in there. The door opens.

"Greta!"

"Yes it is!"

"I cannot believe it is you, where are the girls, are they with you?"

"Do not be silly Seth. You are dead in their minds!"

"But not yours. I could never fool you could I Greta. Greta the know it all. Why couldn't you believe I was dead?"

"Because that was too easy Seth. Nothing really added up as to why you wanted to go southwest instead of northwest as we planned. I do not know why and I want to know why. Why are you dead in your daughter's minds?"

"Why . . . why . . . why . . . you always want answers. Greta, things just did not work out the way I planned and well anyways . . . you never loved me, you just -"

"I did."

"No you really did not. You may have learned to love me but you never loved me like you did Matthew Braummer. And I hated that!"

"You what?"

"Yes and Mr. Braummer was not going to win this one . . . he used to beat me at cards all the time . . . did you know that? However, this time I won! I took the main prize from him and ran! Do not look so confused Greta. He went to Louisiana and I told a lie and married you. We would have stayed out here but I just had to take my prize back home and rub it in!"

"I cannot believe that."

"Well believe it because it is true dear Greta. Unfortunately my other ventures were not doing as well like I said and going to Texas was a great idea."

"What happened to Mr. Cooper?"

"Oh he took a knife meant for me. I knew I could not go back home after that, so I decided since he was now dead I might as well be too. But you could not believe it."

"No I could not. Nothing added up Seth."

"Well I take it you are going to the other cabin with the girls and of course they have all the money. I guess I will have to come back to life and go with you."

""No I do not think so."

"Yes I think so and we can leave right now. I keep things packed and ready to go at a moments notice. This is a moments notice now go out the door . . . we will be one happy family again . . . for awhile."

"No, you do not understand."

"Do tell . . . you married Matt!"

"No . . . that is . . . not yet."

"Oh so he is with you and the girls. This will be good . . . I get to rub it in even more. The lost husband returns."

"You cannot do that to your girls."

"Listen I owe a lot of money to some very mean men and you have the money I need. Call it a welcome home gift. Now . . . outside . . . please. We need to leave right now."

"Why right now?"

"I have been doing a lot of thinking on how to show up at your door step . . . what I would say . . . how I would act. I was planning to leave immediately and now you show up. Makes for a better plan, plus we can still leave immediately."

"I do not know what you think you can gain from this. It will not work."

"Sure it will because this is an even better plan. Now out the door with you. We have a long ride ahead of us."

They mount their horses and begin to ride away from the cabin when a shot is heard. Greta turns to see Seth slumped over on his horse. More shots are fired causing Tilly to rear up and Greta fall to the ground. She looks up to see a group of Mexicans riding toward them. Three more shots are heard, Seth falls to the ground. Greta lies on the ground and looks at Seth thinking; 'Now you are dead to me forever.' She looks in the direction of the Mexicans. Two ride up to her looking at her through their dark squinty eyes. Another shouts to them and they shout back and forth in an unfamiliar language. They approach Tilly, drop her packs and leave. Relief overwhelms Greta and she looks at Seth's lifeless body thinking, 'My God, what did you do?' She then speaks aloud, "I ought to just leave you there for the animals to feed on. However, I cannot. You were, after all, Father to our girls, so I owe you that respect. I will be in need of your coat as the nights are cold up here. And your possibles bag you will not be needing." She drags him to an area to bury him. After setting the final rock on the mound, and placing no marker she says, "Lord I have nothing to say about Seth, except he was a good father to his girls. You knew him best and I suppose you can deal with his short-comings. Amen. Now to think of the living . . . me."

◆◆◆

"Cooper . . . Mrs. Yancey covers her tracks well."

"Yes I see that. And she is running a cold camp. My friend, she is going to be a hard one to track."

"She go to cabin."

"I would like to think that is where she is heading. I know of no other reason for her to go in this direction."

"She is smart. Runs with other horses, walks in water. She part Indian Cooper?"

"No Brave Eagle. Mrs. Yancey was taught by a Trapper. My Mother was right. We are not looking for a woman. We are looking for another Trapper . . . a Mountain Man."

◆◆◆

Greta picks up the packs and carries them into the cabin. "Now I am a foot. Best get a good rest for early leaving." She then realizes Tabby is down the hill. She runs down only to find her gone also. Greta gathers up the bundles and after a few trips, she has everything in the cabin. She then stokes up the fire and replenishes the woodpile.

"Now to get some water while I still have day light. I suppose I follow this path to the water. I hope it is not far. Aaa, good. There it is. Nice little stream. Two bucket full should do just fine. I can fill the canteens for traveling."

The cabin door now closed she lights the lantern on the table. Then turns her attention to the pot hanging in front of the fireplace. "What is in the pot? Stew! Thank you Seth. Let me taste it, yes, of course it is good." She filled a bowl, grabbed a cup of coffee, and sat at the table. Eating the stew she thinks, 'Hum, this is good. Lets see, I taste deer, and rabbit.' She tears some bread and sees something out the corner of her eye. "Well hello there Mr. Mouse. Taking in some warmth from the fireplace I see. So do you come here often? I bet you do for the fact you did not run when I tossed that bread. Enjoy the warmth."

As Greta continues to eat, she begins to look around the room to see if there is anything she may need when she leaves. Next to the door, she had hung the buckskin coat, powder horn, possibles bag, and hat. Next to that a chair with a window above it. Then came a long cabinet with cans of food in wooden boxes. On the far wall a cabinet for the bucket of water to sit on and various large bowls, a small window above. She says, "Mr. Mouse, hear that howling out there? Wolves. Good thing I shut the shutters on the windows and loaded the rifle. We will be safe. Look at you Greta Yancey; talking to a mouse. If anyone heard you, they would think you daft. Well, I have to talk, I have to make sense of all this" She then continues to look around the cabin. After the small window comes a trunk with a lantern on top, a bed along the wall with a trunk at the foot of it. Then space leading to a small woodpile on the wall of the fireplace with a rocker in front of it. The fireplace, then a larger woodpile and back to the door. She sits at a table in the middle of the cabin with two chairs.

"Mr. Mouse . . . this meal was superb. I will take my coffee and relax in that rocker for a while with a piece of spice cake. You know Mr. Mouse, there seems to be a story that goes with this cake that I cannot remember, but I will."

After Greta cleans the table, she takes her coffee, spice cake, and relaxes in the rocker. She thinks, 'This seems like I have done this rocking before, on a porch in the mountains, but not these mountains and not in this cabin. And who is Matt . . . Matthew, a good question. He is handsome man and he seems to know me. Seth even talked of him. Said I loved him. But this Matt left the group, oh well.' She rocks a bit more then says, "Mr. Mouse, it looks to be time for me to build up that fire and turn in. I suspect I will see you come first light. Good night to you Sir and when I leave I will leave some crumbs for you also."

As she lies down she says, "Lord, keep me safe and bring back my memory . . . please. Thank you."

◆◆◆

SAN LOUIE . . .
"Hello Mr. Paarday! How is business?"

Paarday comes around the counter laughing and grabs Matt's hand with a hardy shake saying, "Aaaha, Matyu Braumair. Good to see you again! I tought you in mountains by now. Why you here?"

"Good to see you too Paarday! I had some business to tend to and thought I would head to Earleysburg before the snows hit." Matt says smiling.

"Ah, wee, wee, dee snow can come earrlee in dee mountains. You go see ol' friends ya?"

"Yes. I have to keep them informed as to what is going on. And what better way than a surprise visit."

"Say what you need. I git for you."

"Coffee, sugar, sack flour. . . "

Soon Matt was set to go. He paid Paarday and bid him farewell. The weather was nice and comfortable for mid summer. He spent some time with his friend in Wheeling, Andrew Putman. Who again teased him about Greta. Then on to Earleysburg.

◆◆◆

Back at the cabin. . .

At first light, Greta wakes to a very chilly cabin. Rubbing her arms, she walks over to the fireplace and builds up the fire. Puts the coffee on and in no time, the warmth of the fire begins to fill the room. She goes to the bucket of water pours some in the basin and as she washes her face, the coldness of the water wakes her even more. She dresses and goes to the front door to open it and welcome in the morning light. Instead of a morning sun pouring in its warm rays, she had . . . "Snow? It is too early for snow. How am I to leave now? Mr. Mouse, how do I leave now?"

to be continued. . . .

About The Author

With a Pioneer spirit in her heart and courage to make a difference, Elizabeth continues on the path set out before her. Where other western writers depict females as the weaker sex, Elizabeth shows them to have strength. Not only are they strong mentally, but are able to physically to overcome many obstacles when no man is there to protect and guide them. She takes these women on an adventure that tests them to the breaking point, and when broken, how they come about again in full strength, a strength that can only come from God. Her characters have become heroes in a world of very few, if any.

Her novels, winding around fiction adventure, are known for their accuracy and authenticity of historical accounts. The fact is, not only is it hard to put book down, but also, the reader also experiences a wide range of emotions as they journey through the story. Elizabeth's novels are truly exciting and entertaining.

Some say Elizabeth is following in the footsteps of Zane Grey and Louis L'Amour in her western writings. She however says "I just write a story for others to enjoy." Though at times difficult, she stayed the course with the third book in the GRETA YANCEY SAGA and is working towards the fourth. In the footsteps of these great writers you may see her novels in movie form.

Her drive to write came from moving to Arizona in 1981, where she fell in love with the topography of the West and a taste of what it was once like in the 1700 and 1800's. Life was not easy to live back then, but there was an unmistakable drive and determination to live it to the fullest. Elizabeth traveled the western states and became more enthusiastic with the West and the life one had to live to survive to keep going, yet in a place of breathtaking sunsets, magnificent mountain scenes, and unspeakable prairies, it created a foundation for her writings.

Elizabeth has critiqued novels, poems, poetry books, paintings, and drawings. Her knowledge of writing and art landed her judging positions for various organizations. She spoke at Elementary Schools and Libraries about her books and publishing.

Her strong patience and cheerful attitude allows for quick changes in plans made. And with her husband Jim of 42 years, two married children and six grandchildren, a full time job, changes happen. But still Elizabeth finds the time to write and bring to life wonderful characters. She is also an avid painter. The family attends Lake St. Helen Baptist Church were she is the Sunday school Director and Deaconess. Jim is a Deacon and an In-Home Health Aide, Elizabeth is Manager of the St. Helen Community/Senior Center, both work for Commission on Aging.

When not working or writing, she can be found studying her Bible, baking, painting, playing with her six grandchildren, helping someone or just sitting and visiting with those who happened to drop-in. And they do enjoy drop-in folks. Her welcome mat is always out to greet friends, family or acquaintances who just want to relax and sit a spell.

Elizabeth was born of first generation Polish-American parents, Arthur and Emily Kowalski. She has one older brother, Paul and one younger sister, Rose Marie, making Elizabeth the middle child. She grew up in Sterling Heights, Michigan and now resides in St. Helen, Michigan.

When in High School, she was having difficulty with English and grammar. Her senior English teacher who was a journalist persuaded the other three English teachers to pass her on her writing ability and not on her English and grammar. Elizabeth gives thanks to that teacher who helped her graduate. She has been writing and telling stories ever since.

Through the years Elizabeth not only held Management and bookkeeping/accounting positions, she was also a Cub Scout Den Leader, Brownie Leader, Church Librarian, Chaired the church Ladies Day, and headed other community projects. Elizabeth has taught Ladies Bible Classes, Teen Bible Classes and Acrylic Painting Classes. She and her husband Jim managed Foster Care Homes . . . one for mentally challenged women and the other, years later, for teens and younger children. She co-managed a Drive-In-Theater with Jim being the manager in Algonac, MI. Elizabeth has always loved to bake and sold holiday cookies, Polish pastries, and Wedding Cakes. Just to name a few of her accomplishments.

A very positive woman with a few sayings she lives by:

> With God All Things Are Possible,
> Never Give Up
> Dreams Do Come True.